Children of the Night

Stories

...to read in the dark!!
LoL !!
Enjoy

Children of the Night

Stories

Ulrick Casimir

Corpus Callosum Press

Hastings, Nebraska

Ulrick Casimir

Children of the Night: Stories

Published by: Corpus Callosum Press

Text Design by: Corpus Callosum Press

Cover Design by: Miranda Schmidt

A CIP record for this book is available from the Library of Congress Cataloging-
in-Publication Data

ISBN-13: 978-0-9996869-2-8

Distributed by: Corpus Callosum Press

Hastings, Nebraska

For my mother

Contents

Acknowledgments

I'd like to thank Lee Zacaharias, Michael Parker, the late Tim McLaurin, and John Kessel for helping me learn how to shape stories and sentences. Additional thanks to Jeremy DeForge, Michael Copperman, and Giselle Barone for their more direct assistance with these pieces. A special nod to *Plainsongs* magazine, where a number of these stories originally appeared. Much obliged to Miranda Schmidt for her support, encouragement, creativity, and sharp eye. And finally, I'd like to thank Eric Tucker, editor extraordinaire and just an all-around exceptional and special human being, who tends to get embarrassed by praise . . . though this time, I'm hoping that he will forgive me for it.

Stars of Gold

In lockup, Dennie had never begged God for anything, not once. Not for goods or for paper, not for the type of girl or family who would bother to maintain contact. Not for the love it would take *anyone* to visit after he'd disappointed them all so deeply. He'd bent, sure, in the damp and noisome darkness, same as the other used-up, wadded-up men on his block. Talking to the concrete. Chatting with a God you just *had* to believe was listening.

He never begged, but toward the end he'd arrived at a bargain: Lord, if I find work my first year out, I WILL do good at it, whatever it is. I WILL live past what brought me to this place. Prayers, pleas. Lamentations of the stretch he'd spent in the city—bad decisions, worse mistakes. Ten years of arthritic knees stitched to that prison floor, until finally they earned his plea: Paroled then a job as a hot-dog vendor in his hometown of Brooklyn, handed to him by a sympathetic lesbian barely a month after his release.

Old and dusty memories, Dennie thought, which on this cold and rainy evening went together like some sweet and heady scent in the wind. He had served her quickly, this harried girl. Blond, vanity plates, a bumper sticker that, surprisingly, read "Shaw," the college, in cursive. To-night—the *most* selfish night of the year—and this young girl spoke and moved like a woman with someplace to be, people she loved, folks she missed. Maybe *that* was why she reminded him so much of the way he'd felt in prison.

He'd sped through her order because he could tell she wanted him to, given her directions to RDU without the usual banter, taken her money, counted her change … but there was that scent again, sweet and everywhere, and Dennie began to think of Stella: Tonight, these memories of his were an ache that would not quit.

He'd worked that first job all three years of parole, neither a sick day nor vacation, keeping his promise before heading south, back when most blacks were still running north. He bought his own cart back then, same one that he ran now: Dennie's Coney Island, true boardwalk barkers with *real* trimmings for transplants like him, who were always missing home. But this girl … Dennie breathed deeply, shook his head, smiled, put his hand on hers to calm her. Wished her a happy new year. She blushed and thanked him. He scraped her money into his pouch, sighed, and heard her peel off.

Then he started sausages for three brunettes, maybe seventeen, who snapped their bracelets and touched Dennie's face without asking, and went on about Moore Square, how they were headed there with practically *everybody* (but him, haha!) to watch the Acorn drop. Exact change. They left, and in the dim light and steady rain stood the starched, black uniform of a limo driver.

He was tall, Italian. Short black hair, an engraved wedding band. Street traffic washed in pulses behind him as he shifted foot to foot, working his nose hard with tissue. He crumpled it, jerked a thumb at the rollers. He smoothed a hundred on the counter and said: "One dog, plain and in a hurry. The Man in the car there says you get to keep the change. Except for a dollar, I'm gonna need back one of those."

Dennie finished the order wide-eyed and grabbed the hundred without a word. He tucked it with the big bills in the back of his pouch and pulled a single from the front, the tip that girl had left, and made to hand it over … but then quickly realized his mistake. A $97 tip, yet he couldn't *move*.

In all his fifty-seven years, dead ends and bad situations—even in that hotel room in the city with his little brother twenty-three years ago, too scared to count all that money after the job that would land them both in prison and make Stella disappear—what was this *feeling*? What was that *scent*? He knew now that there really was something in the air. This time, Dennie brought the bill up to his nose, and breathed deeply.

August 7, 1963. Coney Island was clean and bright, a beautiful summer day. Stella Dorchester, a petite girl with a face like polished mahogany, was happiest and prettiest on a boardwalk by a sparkling ocean. He wanted to give her everything, anything, once. *Once*, he thought again, squeezing her hand. *Just once*, and he'd have the cash so they could get married finally, and she'll never need to know where it all came from—

Memories and money, paper trails that are meaningless and peppered with inaccuracy. The ocean *had* sparkled back then, but not with sunlight; there had been plastic things in the waves that day, trash blown down from the walk. And at her best, Stella had been spoiled, moody, selfish. Yet he had loved her more than anyone. Back then, her hand warming his, Dennie had felt something deep enough to convince him that he could get away with anything, up to and including bank robbery.

He breathed in again and shut his eyes. He thought of Stella, Stella and the prison dreams: how he had dreamt not about her but *for* her, on her behalf, as if that could make her wait for his release. His cellmate, Hunky, an immigrant who liked to stretch the truth, had gotten arrested almost as soon as he'd stepped off the flight from Italy. It was any one of a million summer nights, prisoners smoking stale cigarettes, turning currency to ash to sleep and dream like citizens. Hunky in the midst of a story that may not have been true, about a cousin who lived in Brooklyn and spoke little English and still heard "cellar door" as *stella di oro*, and thought that nonsense English phrase the most beautiful thing he'd ever heard.

But before he could remember what was so beautiful about a cellar door, Dennie, for the first time since prison, imagined visiting Stella Dorchester now, after all these years apart. What might happen if he somehow got the address, showed up on her porch this evening, holding a rose that smelled so sweet and soft, his face a glittering ocean, his eyes like stars of gold—

But then he looked at his hands. There was only peach-colored paper there now. The driver had snatched the bill before taking off, leaving only his used tissue for Dennie to throw away.

Many Happy Returns

Peter James grabbed his clicker and dimmed the lights in his office until they scarcely touched anything at all. He sat still behind his desk, then almost immediately stood up and sat upon it. He leaned against his bureau, attitudinized, tracing the oblong burls of its cherry wood: All of this, every painstaking second—all forty-five minutes of it—a desperate attempt to find somewhere within this moment, or in the grain of the wood itself, the patience he knew he'd need for the coming conversation. *Children*, he thought for the hundreth time today: *Who needs them?*

Dusk came quickly, moderating his office's carmine feel with the pale glow of a beautiful moon, yet Peter hardly noticed the change. And now he quit moving altogether and simply stood there in the silence, because he could not stop thinking about his daughter, Marcella, and that goddamned photograph. She would be on her way now, and that sad little snapshot of another girl and her family sat facedown on his desk, atop a stack of freshly prepared stock. Peter walked over now, stared hard again at the back of it. "Surfside Beach, 1985." Eight years ago, and blue ink. Simple information, in the swooped script of a motherly hand.

Peter already knew what he wouldn't tell Marcella. He wouldn't mention he'd had Eddie break the arm of her gynecologist's teenaged son, since she wouldn't say without it why Marcella had been in to see her *three times* in the past month. He wouldn't mention Buss, Marcella's boyfriend of the past six months, the studio photographer who also did high-risk photographic surveillance on contract for both local PIs and the RCMP. This was someone his little girl loved while hardly knowing the guy at all: Peter's eyes strayed again, toward that rotten photograph.

Margaret, his secretary, had drafted and delivered the note he'd dictated, in Marcie's name. Eddie would handle the kid in his own way, and their man at Bell had taken the money to trim those loose ends. *All taken care of …* which was usually a mantra for Peter, as it pleased him to be in control this way. But then he grabbed the photograph again, flipped it over again. He studied its image again, as if he didn't already have every little detail of it memorized.

Emma Cummings. Red hair. Green eyes and lots of freckles. Seventeen, tan and wispy as the beach grass peeking into the frame. To her right stood Roy, the father, and to her left Ruth Anne, the mother. Peter grimaced hard at all three, flicking at the corner of the print with his thumb.

Roy Cummings was a county judge, and he was pulling his kid toward him as if she were all that mattered. And the mother, the eldest in an oil-rich Houston family, with her active open palm blurred above her daughter's shoulder, caught mid-stroke as she waved off what, a mosquito? A midge? Parents of the fucking year, Peter thought, and in the artificial silence of his office he could almost hear this photograph: the sun dropping down behind them, the breeze blowing down the empty beach and through the oil refinery at the horizon, the bars of orange from the sun grinding as they graded the sand.

The first and only time he had ever met Emma, she was a stripper, a junkie, and twenty-three. She was also Eddie's girl. That night, Eddie's birthday, he'd met Eddie and a few of his guys at Marvin's, where Emma worked. And that night Peter did what he should've done, what he always did: He picked up a couple of rounds real fast, then rose to leave ... but then Eddie begged him to stay, and ordered the poor girl to give Peter the works for free.

He'd put out his cigarette; she'd taken his hand. She'd led him through a set of beaded curtains but less than halfway through, Peter was making her stop. He fastened his belt, stuck a big bill in the cup of her bra. He told the girl that she was far too pretty to be doing this, which wasn't true, and then she showed him the back way out and he left and that was it: The one and only time Peter had ever met Emma Cummings, dead or alive. But Peter knew that for the RCMP, this fact didn't and wouldn't matter.

He tossed the photo aside and began flipping through the card stock, each sheet reversibly engrained with more than two grams of product—his latest and least detectable method of running it through the States and into the city. Peter dropped the thick stack with a chunk then slipped across his office to the bar, spinning it open for the mirror inside. She had his dark and even skin, Marcie did, and his hair too, which was a solid natural black, even at fifty. And his gawky length, his penciled-in lips, though paired with her mother's more continental nose.

He lit a beedi expressly because they made his daughter dizzy. He punched the intercom. "Ten minutes, Margie," the smoke drifting in and out of Peter's voice like gravel on a busy walkway. "Gimme that 'n' send her in."

Little Emma Cummings had died a bad death two years ago. Back then nobody cared, not even Eddie, because strung-out strippers die all the time, from Van Nuys to Vancouver they die all the time, and no one cares. But this one's parents did, and Ruth Anne with all her god-damned money. She'd gotten a team of PIs in Texas to work her case and within a year, they'd gotten *both* tox reports, the original and the one Peter's guy at the coroner's had filed in place of it. And then they brought in Donald Morgan, the ex-RCMP PI who saw the names on the reports and put it all together, fast. But with these plans that he and Eddie had made? This too, Peter knew, didn't and wouldn't matter.

So he trained his mind on other things.

He remembered his own daughter at age five. The judo lessons, how Marcie had insisted on taking classes with the boys. *That* was his daughter, or at least the part of himself Peter saw in her. He began to wonder once again why he always double-checked himself before they met. Parsing his own face in a mirror, working through the plan, always a plan, for what he'd say. And tonight she would know what it was, just like she had always known what it was, the one thing he would ever desire that she alone would forever be uniquely qualified to deny him. And while Peter knew this, he knew that Marcie knew it, too. She was his daughter, she knew everything that he did.

Five minutes left.

He lit another beedi, sank into his chair and then stretched out lazily. He watched the legs of his trousers pull over his socks, he took long drags and twirled in his high-back chair, filling the air with bitter smoke. He dimmed his lights even more and stared at the red/white tangle on his marble floor until possession, that pleased and clean sensation, once again smoothed the contours of his mind like a blanket of snow. But then Peter remembered where he was, and looked at his watch.

His office door, easing open. His only child now a silhouette in a black-cherry frame, leaning like the model she was, saying nothing like the mute he'd often wished she were.

"Have a seat," he said, but Marcella did not move.

"It's your mother," her father lied. "She's waiting for us in Vancouver. I'm retiring, out for good. And she wants you and me to meet her there, tonight, for counseling."

*

Rae Jennings pulled away from her boss and went quietly to her own window, stretching as if pulled toward the budding heat of the morning sun.

Three hours from now, she would cover for him one last time. She would take the TTC to Spadina and Dundas and shoot the latest of this month's spate of demolitions, this one of a late-nineteenth-century flatiron being replaced with yet another nameless, faceless office building. Then later, dinnertime, she would head over to the café on Bloor where they often met, where tonight she would finally tell him, Hank Buss, her editor at the *Star*, that they were over.

She would say what she'd been practicing saying these past couple months. There was no one else, and they'd been growing apart: It was useless to keep pretending otherwise. "I'm sorry" is the line she'd rehearsed most, as if briefly apologizing was the most permanent way to say goodbye. But that preparation, that warm-up, felt distant now. Without realizing it, she'd left the heat in her window for the shadow of her own bed.

Late last night, he'd practically begged her not to leave him alone, not this week. To join him drinking that rum he liked so much, to sleep in with him, to shut off her phone. To pretty much stay by his side like a comfort dog, at least through the coming weekend. Hank had gotten to her place well past midnight, in a panic over a shoot he'd done that evening, a ribbon-cutting for a friend of the mayor's on the thirty-first floor of the Entergen building, down Queen Street West. "I'm a fool," he kept hissing, bashing his smartphone in with the flat end of her muddler: "Eighteen-some years," he'd said, "but I should've known. I should've never come back!"

And that was it: No explanation, nothing else, no matter how hard she tried. She hated him, Rae realized, thinking of the busted phone in her sink, the flowers he'd brought with him only to leave them drying on her kitchen counter, and her arms and legs grew cold. He'd wrapped himself in her covers, making it impossible for her to pull much free, and she kept on hating him while he slept, for making her cold, for being so old, for not letting her *be*. Rae rubbed at the stubble on her legs, and turned again toward the light.

Today, the first Monday in August: Caribana, that sea, that tsunami of bodies and color that she had always found so intoxicating and near-impossible to express. Rae remembered her family's summer trips to the city from New York for Caribana, going all the way back to 1993, when she was seven. She remembered sitting on her mother's shoulders at eleven, fumbling with the wheel and button of her dad's old Argoflex Seventy-Five. She'd grown up snapping pictures of the parade, slowly falling in love with this city, but now? Today Toronto felt like when she'd first hooked up with Hank: She wanted that feeling back; she had to leave. She had to leave *him*. She needed to shoot.

Rae slipped her (partial) covers again. Drew her feet up tightly, quietly, and put them flat to the floor. Several minutes later she lay back down, this time on top of the covers, where she fell asleep and dreamt of him: waking, swinging his scarred and spidery legs out from underneath the covers. Standing there completely nude, popping his stiff neck like an aged boxer, running his gnarled fingers through thinning blond hair. Those faded flannel briefs and all the rest of it: everything, as always, with his back to her.

Rae dreamt Hank was leaving and woke to discover that the old man was gone. And so were his roses.

*

Marcella James worked for a house he often shot for, and they'd started sleeping together about a week after their very first shoot. That night, Hank recalled, grabbing a streetcar packed with tourists headed for Chinatown, had felt almost delightfully inevitable.

And in the months after, she had turned out to be witty and sharp. What's more, she talked about her life and her future and it all felt so natural to him, the way she always seemed to automatically include him in the wishful things she said. She'd been vague about her family, sure … but then Hank wasn't hypocritical enough to think that he was in a position to complain. The few times he awoke after she'd already vanished for the day, those were the mornings he despised himself most, all of this lying, necessary as it was, to the person he most wanted to share everything with.

Hank was in love, it had come on fast, and the thing that he feared most had happened the way he'd been worried it might. They finally spent enough time together for Marcie to start with the questions and for him to get sloppy. The double-locked door, the one to the darkroom in his basement: One dry day, Hank went out to fetch her a pack of smokes, leaving Marcie alone at his place, and when he reached the bodega he finally realized what he had just done. The dry air and the metal doorknob of the shop yielded a jolt of static electricity strong enough to prompt a vision of Marcie poking through his briefcase, finding the key she was looking for, slowly and surely sounding the shallows of his trust.

Hank dashed back to his apartment. He leapt up the porch steps and then realized he'd gone the entire circuit without the one thing he'd left for in the first place, her cigarettes. *That* was the moment he decided to do it, set a hard date by which he'd sit his girlfriend down and tell her everything ... despite that telling her anything at all was the one thing he'd promised Donald Morgan he'd never do.

The hard date he'd picked back then was this Thursday, four days from now. Straightforward and brutal honesty, like some tough-love gift, at their six-month mark. So all of this now, how things were and how he felt, Hank admitted as the streetcar ground to a loud and fitful halt, was simply and completely his fault.

He had gotten it late last night, Marcie's letter, but there really was no telling when the thing had been slipped under his front door. Fixer dripped from his fingers and into the fibers of the page, yellowing it in streaks like dribbled sunlight: "I'm sorry," her typed letter said. "Please forgive me ... Marcella."

Four days, he thought for the millionth time. As if she knew, or could've known, or might've known. And *typed*, as if it were Marcie's biggest wish to skewer Hank with the distance he'd automatically created by lying to her. If she could've only waited four days, he thought again ... or if he'd just told her everything up front. But then none of this, not today and not last night, not the past six months, would have felt so incredibly inevitable.

Questions and allegations, regrets and self-recriminations were still ringing in Hank's head when he squeezed from the streetcar and began his quick and pensive lope down Spadina. Chinatown: It was the smell he disliked most, rotting refuse and fried carcasses, greasy duck and sandalwood and unwashed bodies, tangled and coiling from the restaurants at the loose center of the district. The market itself wasn't so bad ... but the tourists. Tourists, Hank decided, are the worst part of *everything*, as the doors to Peking's Wish, where they always met, squeezed shut in a gray thud behind him.

He heard the low sharp sounds of men in a game of mahjong at a corner table, the wheeze and clinks of a distant dishwasher. Otherwise, the flat space before him was quiet as ever. Donald was already at their usual table, his big body flooding a booth, with what looked like chicken and a glass of wine in front of him. He had a purple strip of tapestry for a tie, a tan double-breasted suit, and a pale yellow shirt with coffee stains that reached from button to button. He raised his head as he saw Hank, wiped his hands on a bib and stood, revealing khakis that were an inch too long, over gray suede Brogans that had seen better days, and nights.

Hank walked over, motioned him to sit back down. He breathed in hard, as if determined to hold his breath through what was coming, and slid into the other side of the booth.

Pushing his lunch aside, Donald fanned several snapshots, a map of the marina, and a five-figure check across the table.

*

He took a cab from Chinatown to Marcie's only to find her gone, her apartment totally empty. Between precious sips of lemongrass tea, the landlady explained that last night, the tenant had slipped her key and rent in an envelope through the slot in the office door, and then a moving company had come and no, the girl had not even bothered to leave a number or a forwarding address.

After that, Hank went home and slept. He had portraits needing work, but he *couldn't* work, as sleep was the only thing that beckoned to him now. He shot awake at 2:00 a.m., grabbed his jacket, and hailed a cab. He directed it downtown and told the cabbie to stop at an intersection that he had to repeat. By 3:00 a.m., Hank was loping aimlessly into the heart of the financial district, with its utility poles and skyscrapers picking at the meat of an empty, endless night.

A subway train rattled, wobbling the ground beneath him and filling Hank with an intense and grinding blend of fear, anxiety, and ... dislocation? But this was not Marcie now, this feeling. Couldn't be, although perhaps this was Marcie met with something else. Something bigger, something *more*.

Hank reached Queen Street West and saw the remains of a large liquor warehouse that had been torn down last year, for condos that had yet to be built. A distant amber light played through the rubble, making shadows of the skeleton of a floor ripped to shreds. Steel reinforcements, the remains of blasted concrete, kept clawing, pulling, twisting at the night. Three silhouetted alley cats gave chase to one another under yellow tape, through the blue barriers beyond them.

Hank flagged another cab and quickened his pace; he needed to stop by the marina before heading home. He reached the cab and turned around for one last look at the ruins of that warehouse, and from this new angle found the source of that amber glow: one single distant traffic light, a steady signal of caution.

*

Another day or two of dead ends finally led Hank to conclude what anyone else would have days before: The woman he loved was gone, and she was never coming back.

She hadn't called, stopped by, anything. He still had stuff that she had left at his place, but he'd stopped hoping she would return for her belongings and give them a chance to talk things through, or at least for him (or her) to advance explanation. When he slept, which was often, Hank felt as if he were floating in fickle currents, drifting loose-limbed in unpredictable tides and eddies, uncertain whether he should swim to shore or wait to be spit up there. He still didn't know whether to call the RCMP or an old girlfriend.

It was 8:00 p.m. sharp on Friday, the night Donald had indicated in his instructions, and Hank was in a lawyer's suit and tie. In his breast pocket were several rolls of Ilford HP5 that he could push hard then agitate while processing, for good contrast and grain without the betrayal of a flash. His brown leather camera bag, identical in appearance to an office satchel, held a 500 mm mirror lens at 2.8 that he'd shortened and further customized to fit the Leica doubler beneath it. Flush against those, an 80-200 mm zoom that he always packed just in case something brought him close. At the bottom of the main compartment was the Leica body, quietest one they made, with a mount he'd machined to take the lenses. The satchel's side compartment held the same portable tripod that his mother had bought him secondhand about a decade ago, when he was sixteen, and under it sat the small-caliber pistol, a Berreta 92s, that Donald had given Hank last year for Christmas.

He'd visited this city alone right after finishing college, Hank had, and he immediately knew that he wanted to move here, that more than anything in the world he wanted to make his living charting the pulse of this place, and taking detailed snapshots of its insides. Instead, he now made money by shooting the prettiest parts of its skin, and the foulest reaches of its underbelly. Once upon a time, he'd wanted to make Marcie a permanent part of his life. Instead, six months in, the woman had become a permanent part of his memory. Everything, Hank decided, that was good and clean had turned out to be fleeting or unreal. He was still thinking this when he walked into the gutted-out ground floor of the Interprov building.

The rooftop was cluttered with large HVAC units, two of which Hank knew he could kneel between and shoot, unobserved, at a forty-five-degree angle to the east, from the south side. He'd scouted this building; his job was to take pictures of the same cocaine trafficker and Peruvian lowlives that he'd been shooting around the city for months, this time during a meeting in a boat moored at a pier about twenty-five yards from the Interprov's ground floor. Donald had questioned whether the rooftop was safe to shoot from, since the RCMP had cordoned off the grounds, and the demo company had stripped the thing for its implosion on Sunday. But they'd agreed: That sightline was just too perfect to resist.

With a penlight, Hank wound through the mezzanine and up twenty pitch-black flights, to the top floor. He stepped down a hallway lit orange by the setting sun, which came aslant through windows of offices with their blinds, doors, partitions, and fixtures removed. He found the ladder to the roof, disabled the padlock, and hoisted his satchel up and out onto the cool gravel, with about forty-five minutes to spare.

He made his way to the space between the two largest HVAC units, pulled out his tripod, and placed it so that the doubler and lens would go no further than the edge of the roof. He screwed the body to the tripod, loaded the camera. He attached the doubler and the lens, and then he leaned against the unit at his right, to keep gravel from punching into his knee.

Even from the map, Hank had been able to tell that he would be shooting from virtually over the water. He looked down into Lake Ontario, and then at his watch. Thirty-five minutes left, zero activity on the boat. The last golden bit of sky shimmered, and the boat-tour operators out on the lake kept pointing at the sunset mirrored in the gilded windows of the building below him.

Hank looked at the water again, this time at the sparkling reflections playing across it. He tracked flotsam and jetsam floating in it.

He waited.

*

At 8:35 p.m., roughly thirty-five minutes after they had watched the photographer snake through the barricade and enter the ground floor of the building, Eddie and two of his boys tracked down the leads running up the support columns to primer charges over high explosives, which were positioned along those steel columns on the first, seventh, fourteenth, and nineteenth floors. Eddie, who held the radio-controlled detonator, went up the main stairwell of the building, quietly climbed the ladder to the roof and then, under cover of the humming HVAC units, padlocked the trapdoor that led outside. After that, he jogged down to the ground floor and checked his watch.

They had synchronized their timepieces beforehand. At 8:50 p.m., they all met in the lobby and then the two other men left Eddie behind, to make sure they got a decent table for three at the Fran's six blocks north. At 9:05, Eddie would meet them there for a cappuccino, and when they finished, they would shake one another's hands and go their separate ways, quietly retiring for the night.

*

It was 9:00 p.m., and Hank was getting jumpy. These meet times could be a little off, but they were never too early. He gave up his cover and began to look around. He peered over the rooftop, then ran for the trapdoor and tried it. He panicked, he felt a sway and rumble beneath his feet and out of instinct, out of sheer desperation, Hank sprinted across the rooftop toward the lake.

And before he knew it, he was in the air: jumping from the rooftop a split second before the building below him came tumbling down, barely capable of imagining that he would hit the water, twenty impossible stories below him, alive.

Hank could feel everything else falling as he fell. He heard the invisible sirens screeching, saw the red and blue lights yet to come winding through the night sky, encircling the base of a building that was no longer there, on his way down.

The black surface of the lake should have grown in size. Instead, it became a postcard-sized screen for a small projector: He watched the wet trip to his apartment to grab essentials, after stopping at a payphone nearby to ring Donald and tell him what had happened. He saw Donald—not just his client, his *friend*—meeting him at a street corner near Donald's home, the big man using small and colorful words, even while thanking God that Hank was still alive. He saw the orange-and-blue morning sky through the window of Morgan's spare bedroom, as he waited for the sun to rise and set again. Planning destination after destination, all the same, away from here.

Wherever Marcie was, whomever she was with, whatever she was doing, she would be OK ... and so would he: The lake itself, the thing that made this city, was telling him so. There they were, and they were there, him and Marcie. Alive yet dead to one another, living lies on the opposite sides of a moving screen that kept burning, burning—

*

The boat stayed empty. Those men, they never came.

One building came down and fifty-seven hours later, police and fire investigators found within the ruins the surprisingly intact remnants of highly customized camera equipment, but nothing like the crushed bits of a corpse.

One week after the implosion, Marcella shuttled back from Vancouver to find her dad in a vile way—so different from the conciliatory man who'd repented for all past sins just days before. Anyway, Vancouver: like an acting workshop, the saccharine slime the whole visit had left on her tongue.

She called Hank Buss *again*, for what had to be the fiftieth time since she'd gotten back, this time from a payphone at the airport ... and found his line had gone from "busy" to "disconnected." She ran by his place, which was totally cleared out, then spent that weekend, day and night, distraught and confused. By Monday, she was searching the city for him with PIs provided by her father, who just couldn't stop apologizing for his recent attitude. For several consecutive months those pricey PIs tried, finding nothing.

A grade-two concussion. Fractured left femur, broken right ankle. A badly wrenched neck and back. Hank lasted long enough in that water for an elderly couple, rich vacationers from Michigan, to scoop him out. They called an ambulance from the phone on their sailboat. He gave the paramedics Donald's son's name instead of his own, made sure he dropped his wallet into the water as they transferred him to the gurney, and then had someone call Donald's home phone from the emergency room at Wellesley. By the time Donald arrived, Hank had passed out from the drugs and the raw pain of the doctor and those nurses setting his leg and ankle. The next morning, Donald wheeled his young friend onto his flight, and he implored the kid never to return to this city.

Dominica, in the Lesser Antilles: the "nature island of the Caribbean," a place Hank had learned enough about to know that he could lose himself there shooting, cheaply and for a very long time. While Marcella and Peter were organizing half of Toronto to find him, while the RCMP were investigating the demolition company to find out how it was possible for a building to come down on its own and two days early, Hank was recuperating in Mahaut in his wheelchair, weighing the many different ways to shoot black sand beaches using color slide film, and imagining the gear he'd need for those yellow crags of sulfur in Soufriere.

A year passed, during which the condos at Queen Street West were never built—Entergen & Associates, Peter's new shell company, eventually erected an office building there in its place—and Marcella gave up completely on finding her missing boyfriend. By then her son, named Henry after his father, was five months old, and Hank had left Dominica to assist the Kingston Police Department in Jamaica for a spell.

*

A few years later, while again visiting Dominica, Hank bumped into a woman who wore a bright and multicolored dress with no hat. Her face was dark, heavy with lines, and when she placed her hand on his belly and proclaimed, in patois, that this was the only person she had ever met like this, so alone and so un-dead, Hank shrank away from the woman as if she were evil.

But then she looked up at the sky and pointed. And the place of her birth, the same island she'd often tried to leave, to which she'd always seemed destined for many happy returns, somehow it now felt so brand new. And the whole new thing began to dance beneath the woman's feet.

The white man was gone now. He'd scampered away like some persecuted manicou and so she stood in the middle of the narrow busy street and looked again, at the sky, and there it was: sunlight like you've never seen before, a thousand bursting bulbs like from the old-time cameras. Like an orchid and a sunflower, a buttery tangle that ended in blue space, and skittering vapor. She gave in to this feeling, she began to spin with her arms outstretched, at this light that was pure and unblinking, that felt endless, and so *alive*—

Just Like Me

On a Monday morning in late spring, the Reyes brothers fell into a pair of those fan-shaped chairs that often line the façades of coffee shops across the city. The Owl Bowl, the gray-brick building where the brothers were, anchors the northwest corner of Clancy and Templeton, twin two-lane blacktops that make an upturned "T" at the eastern edge of town. Four ill-placed utility poles wrapped in handbills and posters have always marked that intersection.

Ninety-eight-pound Tino flopped into his chair then played at breathing like their fat Uncle Luis. Little brother Tony soon followed suit, until both were laughing like maniacs. Tino wiped at his forehead, twice, yet his jet-black bangs stayed where they were.

Tony rolled the bottom edge of his glass in circles across the table. He smoothed his hair, successfully, from his forehead back.

"It's so hot today, bro," Tony said, still smiling. "Maybe we should go to school. At least they got AC."

"Hey," Tino said, no longer smiling. "Go right ahead."

"Man, I don't want to get busted again. All that trouble for what?"

"Yeah?"

"Yeah."

Tino said nothing, checking his phone.

Tony sighed, shook his head. He sipped at his water and looked out at the utility poles. He wondered how hard it would be for Tino, once he got a license and if he ever got a car, to see around those things. He thought they looked a lot like the totem poles he'd learned about last year in school ... except these ones got more boring higher up.

An hour went by, during which the sun chewed up their shadows, but they didn't move. A single Mercedes in an imperial shade of cream shot by, westbound on Templeton Avenue. Tino pointed at the car and called it a penis-mobile. Tony thought about going shirtless but decided against it.

Tuesday

Noon came and went and the heat kept rising, leaving one cottony billow in that pale sky. Cars and trucks whirred down Templeton Avenue.

"You guys gotta buy something," the manager said. "If you're gonna sit here, read the sign. These chairs are for Owl Bowl customers only."

But the brothers ignored him, kept on watching the sky. Tony was thinking the sun was dodging this cloud, while Tino was wondering whether that cloud, the only visible trace of moisture, was running for its life from the parched lips on his face—

"Hey. Gentlemen. Did you hear me?"

"Yeah," they both said. "We fucking heard you."

"We'll buy some shit," Tony said, "you don't fucking worry."

The old black man shook his head and went back inside. Tino glanced at his little brother and raised one hand, rubbing his fingertips together.

Tony sprung a plastic wallet from his pocket. "Two dollars," he counted.

"Ain't shit."

They turned at the sudden racket of an old engine, saw a white van perched at the corner on Clancy. The driver hadn't bothered with his signal, but from the way he was angled, the Reyes brothers knew that he was taking a right.

A gold BMW shaped like the *Argo* itself coursed down westbound Templeton. The driver of the van let off the brake before he thought to look around the utility pole at his left.

The van chirped. The Bimmer hugged and traced Templeton, until both car and street dipped into the sky.

The driver waited for the car to disappear then looked around, all directions, before pulling onto Templeton and parking in front of the boys. He jumped out of the van; he shook his thick black hair in the hot breeze.

Tino's mouth drew. He looked down, at his T-shirt: Phil Anselmo, mid-salute. Tony smoothed the fourteen words in black text on his white shirt. The older boy was practically licking his lips by the time the driver strolled around the front of the van.

He wore tan work boots with orange mud caked on the soles, dark-blue jeans that were white at the knees, crosshatched front and back with grease and dirt. His white sweat-stained T-shirt read "Viva España" in green cursive across the front; he had the big, rough hands and chipped yellow fingernails of a bricklayer.

He looked up, smiled at the Reyes brothers, and kept walking. "¡*A la chingada*!" Tino said, as the driver strode past them.

He froze with his back to the boys. He turned and Tony slipped forward, balanced on the balls of his feet.

"*No soy Mexicano*," said the driver before going inside.

Wednesday

Four blocks down Templeton, a tired man in a fluorescent green vest tried hard to control a jackhammer. The noise it made would have forced the boys inside, if the humidity and rain hadn't dampened the sound.

Workers quavered in the distance. Rainwater on the street raised thick oils to the surface of it. Tino rubbed his hands against a white T-shirt that was two generations old and read "KOOL" in green bubble letters. Tony wore a white T-shirt with ripped-off sleeves and little elasticity.

They'd arrived armed with $6.05 in change that Tino found in the bench seats of their mother's Chevy Nova. Tino got an iced mocha latte. Tony had to settle for a tiny cup of coffee.

Tino started pushing around the pearly cubes at the bottom of his cup with his straw and got so distracted that he almost missed the van that was, once again, parking in front of them. He raised his eyes, grinned, lit one of his mother's cigarettes.

The man jogged around the front of the van, smiled in recognition, then wrinkled his face, fanning at the smoke.

"Amigo," he said. "Boys your age should not be smoking."

Tino took a drag, stood up, and blew it in the man's face.

Knots of muscle flashed along the man's jaw. Tony moved forward, ready for anything ... which is when the man's demeanor completely changed. He smiled a big smile in Tino's direction.

"You live not three trailers down from me."

"No you don't," Tino said. "We do not live anywhere near any goddamned Mexicans."

"Yes we do," the man said. "There are many Mexicans in our trailer park. You're in high school with my son. Your mother, she's a kind of a Puerto Rican lady, and you guys have been there a year maybe?"

"*No.*"

"*Sí, es cierto.* And your father. He's a bricklayer. Just like me."

The older boy's vision bled, and his feet moved faster than he expected: He stumbled fist-first toward a spot in the air where the man's face had been.

A Lexus, black and feline, zoomed down Templeton, westbound. The car's factory-tinted windshield and windows mirrored the Owl Bowl, rendering the scene there in a crisp mélange of pinks and blues.

The sixteen-year-old Metro atop Clancy looked held together with invisible tape. The driver flicked and tugged the turn signal to get it to flash, pulled an unassisted wheel to his right, and took the utility pole to his left at face value.

Tino fell into the man, who caught the boy's fist and spun him around. Tony moved like hot air around him, bit hard into his back, and pummeled his crotch from behind.

The driver of the Lexus stared at the melee through his rust-colored windshield. The driver of the Metro gaped through the rain, let his foot off the brake, and inched from Clancy onto westbound Templeton. The sound of the jackhammer diminishing. The wind picking up, the bright flashes of clouds and metallic clashing: all that heat and water, pounding in the air.

Children of the Night

Be yourself but within reason: This is what he remembers while snorting a half-packet of powder at the side of an unpaved road, the one behind the house that, in the 1970s, belonged to a police chief still renowned for making Sanford somewhat respectable. Tru, his favorite of the hamlet's limited selection, is massaging his chest with her hands while working his lap as if it were Halloween. The juice, the location ... being with her, BJ had explained before he paid, was more exciting that way.

Be yourself but within reason: It was what his parents had said that Sunday morning seven years ago, echoing warnings they'd been giving him all his life, as they neatly, metaphorically, tucked the last corner of their Volvo wagon in onto itself. Buttoned down the car full of things as if it were a pocket made of rubber and steel, and then drove well below the speed limit the one hundred and forty miles from Wilmington to the university to help their son move into his first dorm room. Two black Shakespeare scholars, and parents, who had met in the late 1970s: His mother, sitting in the passenger seat reciting lines from scene 3 of act 1 in *Hamlet*, making an intellectually, tremendously sad and self-conscious joke. His father, who'd begun parsing picture-less manuals on kids the day that his son was born, leaning forward with the intensity he'd maintained in raising his child, his *only* child, to be a good and clever lad, to be himself ... just within reason.

Within reason. This bit was the part that BJ had repeated to himself, being a terribly shy kid, bookish and clever. A university freshman at sixteen. Analytical. Cerebral. Effete and ineffectual; blind to the real power of world/word choice until the middle of his senior year, when he finally realized that it wasn't so much *reason*—it was *limits*, be yourself but within *limits*, that they'd truly meant. And to make things worse, he'd been the last person in the world to figure this out.

Hard and distant, the full moon floats like glass in the pines, making tight circles of the black needles in the trees. Tru quits, reapplies hot-pink lipstick, she shoves his dirty crinkled bills into her noisy purse. She grunts that she'll walk and she slams the truck door shut and he turns the key, and flips on the radio. Rolls the dial quickly, stopping at the kind of air where the Doobie Brothers are always begging you to listen to the music.

A bird of indeterminate hue and shade flits expertly, fluttering within those sharp needles ... and BJ watches until it shoots out and disappears. He zips his fly, he lights a cigarette. He rides the speed limit in shaky waves, back to his little apartment on the other side of town.

*

The legend literally read "Brick Capital of the World." But to Charlie Bujold, parked now in his wheelchair next to his bedroom window, that legend had *really* said "Opportunity for Change," the promise of renaissance encapsulated at the tip of his finger, in the name and the population and the meaning within that factoid, printed (as it were) in a brick-red bulleted list: *Sanford.*

He placed the map on his lap and reached down, touching the metal wheels of his chair. He'd spent the day thinking that now was as good a time as any for him to forgive himself and so he stood, from the wheelchair in which he'd been planted these past couple of years. Folded the map, stuck it in his back pocket. He slipped the wedding ring from his arthritic finger and into his dresser.

Charlie ambled down the carpeted hallway, step by creaky step and into his brown and dusty living room. Yes, he thought briefly and for the millionth time, he could've slowed down that rainy night two years ago, instead of speeding and laughing like a maniac at his wife's dumb idea of tact. He could've slowed down then ... but he daren't stop himself now. One foot in front of the other. Time had come for him to forgive himself.

When Charlie allowed himself to remember his dead wife, he also automatically recalled his grandmother, his father's mother. Two sweet yet bitter, gloomy women who, when he thought about it, were almost exactly the opposite of his daughter Belize. Charlie reached the end of the hallway and ran his tongue across what he knew to be the zygotic stage of a boil above his left incisor. He then tapped his teenaged daughter on her shoulder and said, speaking aloud for the very first time since the accident:

"Start packing, B. We're moving to Sanford."

Charlie looked at his daughter, satisfied. The way she'd done her hair up today, tied in two tight pigtails ... he knew that she did this because it reminded her of her mother ... and then just like that, it was back to Grandma Bujold. Those boils, forming at the upper edge of his gums: The last time he'd suffered from them was forty-four years ago, the same day he'd done his part to put the old lady in the ground.

Charlie had been the first to find her that summer, the frozen scarecrow hunched up in her own daybed, below a French window through which the sun poured in each morning and made Roxbury not-so-bad a pocket of the city for an hour at a time. This was 1974, and his grandmother was, Charlie thought, still sleeping at 9 a.m. And she must've fallen asleep something hard, too, because this was a woman utterly opposed to sleeping anywhere but in her own damned bed.

Probably just got tired, is what he'd thought back then. Tired of looking for the cloth necklace he'd snatched from inside her Bible and hid upstairs in the bathroom, to let her know what he already knew to be true (chiefly from hearing his mother say it): That Grandma didn't need to sleep while wearing a stupid cloth necklace to keep from waking up in Hell. Little Charlie grinned. He shook her arm, and yelled for help.

Those boils … they'd shown up at the funeral, where Charlie had played his tongue across them, doing any quiet thing he could to take his mind off Grandma Bujold in that box and in that dirt. She'd been wearing the necklace to bed every night for seventeen years, her idea of insurance, was what his parents whispered as they stood alongside him under an oversized umbrella, two things Charlie had not known with that kind of precision and that got him thinking: Boils, in his mouth, four feet above ground. Two adults and a child standing in a sludge of brown ochre, mourning an old black woman who (Charlie was piecing it together) had died from fear of dying—

The following night, his mother peered into his mouth, paused for a minute, grimaced, and then pronounced those little bumps to be the onset of thrush. His father yelled and sent Charlie to the bathroom, to take a hard look in the mirror, for a boy his age should not be taking pennies and used-up gum from the streets and sidewalks and putting them in his mouth. Charlie tried to explain that pennies smelled nasty, that he hated gum, that only babies got thrush. His machinist of a father stood listening within arm's reach, running one fat thumb across the silver buckle of his cracked, leather belt.

So Charlie had done it. He'd taken that long hard look at himself, in a bathroom where this was not easy given how petrified he was of opening the medicine cabinet. He hadn't really known what the necklace meant when he had hidden it. But he knew insurance, that heavy word, possibly the heaviest thing he could imagine. He held his breath, flung open the cabinet. He flushed the necklace; he watched it wind its way from his sight and into the sewer—

And still they grew.

Those boils, hovering beneath his upper lip, at times like a clipped fingernail jammed under the surface of his gum, at others a stinging reminder of an unspeakable crime, one that was still gestating within the creases of his imagination. He'd killed his own grandmother. He'd killed his *Grandma*: Charlie cried, a lot, silently and on his own, in the quiet of his bedroom, through hot summer days and the cool moonlight that blanched his bed, until early one morning he snuck out, found a Catholic church he'd never been to, and slid into an open confessional booth, where he bayed with all his heart (to a priest who could not stop giggling) that he was sorry, that he would never again touch another blessed spatula.

God had forgiven him, because God was God and so God had to. Those were the rules and all that was left, Charlie knew, was for him to forgive himself. So he went home and late that same night, on his knees in front of his bedroom window, staring down the winking orb of the moon, the boy made penance. He remembered his grandmother, fondly: her sense of humor, how if she'd lived, she would've gotten the joke. By morning, the boils had receded and Charlie knew, without a doubt, that this had happened because he'd forgiven himself. And now, standing here in front of Belize, he realized that by tomorrow, these new boils would be vanishing, too.

"Start packing," etc. was the first thing he'd said to anyone, including his daughter, these past twenty-two months and he was *standing*. So imagine Charlie's shock at his teenage daughter's total lack thereof. She only stood, matching his height, and brushed his upper lip with two fingers. She told him he had new gray growing in his whiskers, which caught him so off guard that he didn't say anything back.

But Belize was, Charlie reminded himself for the zillionth time, warm and brilliant. She had taken *great* care of him these past two years. She would graduate in a couple days, too, top of her class. A big-time reader, an aspiring screenwriter. A seventeen-year-old, much-improved, kinder version of her very own mother—

*

Highway One, at least the bone of it hung between Raleigh and Sanford, belies its muscular hedging: cockspur hawthorn big enough to keep anything but insects at a distance; poison oak wound round the base of huge, billowing oaks trimmed back from that doubled-up and divided, ever-hungry line of thought. And it keeps going, it just keeps going, this highway, like a dart you've thrown in the night, and you don't miss the night until the oaks that crowded it are no longer there.

Scrub grass. Long tough pulls of it. Bleached hard by daylight, yellow in this summer moon. This is the drive that goes south and west: Pine trees marching, thinner than ever, and blacker too. Needles wheezing in the moonlight, sharp and bloody, the air in this car getting stickier by the minute. And those hedges, telling her eyes to keep out, yet they just keep straying in.

"Hot," is what he says, breaking a silence that he didn't fully understand, and she thinks, for the millionth time: Like a fart in the wind. "Ain't it?"

"Huh-nuh."

And then he says, "Nice night though. Times like this, Mom and I used to wish we had a convertible, so we could take it to the beach. And we could sit in the back and eat cheese and drink wine or whatever, and watch the moon come down until it reached the water. You know, that kind of thing."

Once again: "Huh-nuh."

"Well, maybe we can trade this heap in for a convertible when we get to Sanford. I read online they have real cheap cars there. Lord, your Mama. What a beautiful woman. Thank God we left you at home. You know, some people think seat belts won't save them from anything. But I'm walking, talking proof that ain't true. I mean, I was wearing mine, right? And she wasn't wearing hers. I'm alive, and your mother ... well, I guess on second thought, maybe she could've been driving. Or maybe she could've moved ..."

"Dad," she says.

"Yes, dear?"

"You forgot your pill. You need water, too. Here, why don't you just have a little sip of mine?"

*

Belize Bujold's earliest memory was a dream of her own birth. Her parents had been—until two years ago—dreams to have as such; she had never been able to watch the nightly news straight through because of the encroaching effect the plights of others typically had upon her dream-like existence. If dreams had played the biggest part in keeping the girl sane these past couple years, then it was a nightmare that had given her the ability to brush her father's whiskers and experience zero surprise at him standing and talking, after years of absolutely nothing.

For twenty-two months straight, every night, she had dreamt of her mother and father as a single inseparable unit, and this had kept the girl moving, illuminating her steps and making the chores forced upon her, by a grown man who refused to stand or speak, less real and more tolerable. And in these dreams, there was her mother and there was her father, one frequently melting into the other … *No worries*, they seemed to say: *Things can only get better*. Once upon a time, in the absence of a father to guide her, a fifteen-year-old girl decided the memory of her parents together would be more than enough to live off of, and so she moved on.

She had changed his bedroom slippers. She had dragged him, and his wheelchair, up and down the carpeted staircase. She had run off the door-to-door salesmen when they asked to see the man of the house. She had forged his signature on checks, letters from the insurance company, school documents, policies. She had put her dream of becoming a Hollywood screenwriter on hold, had led his life for him simply because he was her father. He was her father, and even if he wasn't being a good father now he'd been a good father way back then—this is what those dreams had reminded her. And she had decided she would let him grieve in his own way, for as long as the man needed to, because deep down she was thankful that the accident hadn't taken him, too.

But the week before he'd decided to rise up and walk and talk like a man again, Belize began to reconsider the past in a way that made her more anxious about her own future than she had ever been. They were studying Descartes and Sir Thomas More in school, perhaps that was it, what made her selfish enough, finally, to wonder if it might be possible for her to dream not *about* the past, but *into* the future. The night before she brushed her father's whiskers with her fingers, Belize had gone to bed with the intention of injecting herself into her own imagination. To try once more to dream the future, to see what might've happened if her parents hadn't hit a patch of water in the rain. If her mother hadn't met a telephone pole headfirst, at seventy-seven miles an hour.

But when the girl closed her eyes that night, she saw something she didn't expect: the truth. Suddenly there was only one real reason why her mother would've ever left her at home alone in the first place: they'd been fighting. Only one word that would ever have caused her sometimes irritable and excessively Catholic father (who had told her once of how he'd learned to drive in Boston, during one of the worst winters in history) to race down a rain-soaked highway. Mom, Belize finally understood, had wanted a divorce. And who in hell could blame her?

Not Belize. Certainly not after these past two years, watching him be self-serving enough to strip her of the one thing that she could never rebuild or regain. Not that she wasn't to blame; fact was, she had *overdone* her job, and if he expected her to wait on him, hand and foot, for the rest of his miserable life, skip her college commencement and pick up the certificate afterward like she'd just done for her high school graduation—

It wasn't his heart medication that she'd handed him just now, but a sleeping pill shaped so close he could never tell the difference, a trick she'd learned a year ago. She could give him *anything* and he wouldn't know. Soon he would be fast asleep and she could drive and cry and think about her life without having to think *for* her own father first.

They hit Sanford. Inched along a dirt road until they arrived at the back door of their new home, a moderate-sized yellow thing with a dishwasher and a small front porch. The house that, Belize would soon learn, used to belong all through the 1970s to a Sanford police chief still regarded as the man who'd succeeded in making the town respectable.

*

That first Sunday evening, a month after they'd moved in, crickets whirring, nothing moving. Thick summer air, Belize thought, dulls the sound at night. Maybe that's why she hadn't heard gravel moving, or punching at tires; maybe it was why she wasn't now hearing the noises that she had always believed accompanied such actions as she was observing through space and panes of glass, her kitchen window and the windshield of the truck. Belize stood there in the dark with her college brochures in hand, wishing it were winter. Maybe then, she would've at least been able to *hear*.

Ten minutes since she'd first noticed it, the truck, which was red or green or brown, anyway it looked black in the light of the moon, with its engine stopped. Five minutes had elapsed since she saw Tru, one of the few girls Belize had met so far in town. Sweet, pleasant, pretty, and unassuming Tru: She had scampered in her tight top and miniskirt up the dirt road, and jumped into the passenger side of the truck. Within moments her torso had disappeared.

Belize dropped the brochures on the counter. She snuck around the pine trees, threaded through shadow, careful yet amazed at what she imagined she might do if she did get spotted. Twenty yards from the truck, in the shade of the overgrown oak on the other side of the road, far enough away to see and not be seen, so motionless that she thought she heard a single bird flapping its wings. The guy grunted, Belize smirked at that.

Tru raised her head into view and stuffed something into a shiny purse. She then slammed the truck door shut and left the way she came, on foot. A flame flared inside, vanished, and then the truck itself fired with a groan, then eased away.

*

HER: No. I want *you* to read it, aloud. Please?

HIM: OK, Jeez. Is your dad really asleep?

HER: Oh, trust me. Creep's asleep.

HIM: Promise you won't make fun of me? It's just, it's the first thing I've written down in a really long time, and it's not—

HER: (palming his cheek) Just read. *Aloud.*

HIM: (reading) "Dear Mom and Dad, everything is fine. It's been a year since that summer, and Raleigh. When I woke up high and found a note that I had written, taped to my bathroom door. 'Try and find me,' it said, but Raleigh is a real big town …"

*

—in her father's kitchen, three months since Belize first asked him to come to her like a warm summer rain, and he'd done just that. Sitting on the counter next to the sink, he grabbed her head and pulled it hard to his chest, as if she could hear the source of his words over the practiced in-and-out of his breathing.

He wanted her entirely, but that wasn't it. He wanted her to understand his gratitude, but that wasn't it, either. He wanted her to know that she made it simple and clean and good to want this now and the next thing later, but that was not, could never be enough. He matched his inhalations to the throbbing in her chest, he remembered that she was four years younger than he, that her teenaged heart would outlast his beaten, battered lungs by at least the concomitant number of seconds, minutes, hours, months, and years.

Sure: He had walked back that first night because he had seen her shadowy outline in the trees and had noticed something else, beyond the limits of sight and quite possibly imagination. Not that he could ever tell her this, but a bunch of doves had spun from the top of her head and into the trees, and that's the kind of thing that just doesn't happen every day and is often referred to as a "sign." Only the last thing he wanted was some religious bullshit clogging this up.

He'd pretended his ride had broken down, that he couldn't find the phone he'd deliberately left in the truck.

She pretended that she was letting him in just so he could use their landline to call a friend. BJ dialed his own number, spoke to the ringing in the handset, told it not to worry, that he'd call a cab. He returned to the kitchen, where she showed him the short script that she'd been writing before flinging herself upon him, swallowing his tongue, telling him that he didn't need to do what they both knew that he was doing, and for some reason, perhaps because he was simply ready to, he believed her. She made him promise, swear, to keep returning to her on a weekly basis.

She had, all last month, drugged her father to a stupor then stopped by BJ's apartment. She had risked her life by staying the night when the craving sunk its barbs into his skin. She had kept him from ripping out his eyes or, worse, taking another hit. Except for some pink, pimple-sized scars, remnants of speed rash along the white line marking the top edge of his upper gum, withdrawal had left BJ unscathed.

Recovery cannot be that simple, he thought, sitting in her kitchen while her idiot father dozed upstairs, just like every other night—"Dear Mom and Dad," he read aloud, cupping his girlfriend's small tight breast with his free hand, "everything is fine. It's been a year since that summer, and Raleigh. When I woke up high and found a note that I had written, taped to my bathroom door."

BJ finished, and looked at Belize. Her eyes were closed, the early autumn moonlight making the pink of her T-shirt an indeterminate shade of gray, and the tone of her skin, her long arms and slender face, into the mottled, muted tones of cigarette ash. *God* he loved her. Though he wondered briefly if he hadn't simply replaced one dope with another.

In front of Belize, on the bar, in the center of the kitchen, sat a crinkled map. The United States, with a red diagonal line drawn east to west, bending, vanishing deep into the shoulder of southern California.

"Remember," Belize asked after a while, "around three months back? That first night? You drove to the end of the dirt road, parked, walked back, told me you blew a tire? That you had to call a friend?"

"It was," BJ said. "And I did."

"And you saw me in the shadows of the trees?"

"There were these doves above your head. A flight of 'em. You told me that they were playing in the trees like children in the night."

"Yeah, there's a nest up there somewhere," she said, and she pointed to what he'd just read. A letter to his mom and dad that had evolved into something else, something that they would better understand. More story than epistle.

"This is good," Belize said. "And there's nothing now, nothing but me," and BJ nodded and massaged her breast more deeply.

"You need to send this to them," she said. She took his hand from her breast, pressing his index finger to her lips. "Do that tonight and we'll leave tomorrow afternoon."

"Sure, baby. You know, whatever."

Belize dropped BJ's hand. She pulled a green pill bottle from the pocket of her jeans: Charlie's nitroglycerin, with a couple tadalafil tabs mixed in. She'd bought them from BJ's former dealer then scraped off the color, buffing them down so it would be impossible for him to tell the difference, not until it was way too late. She stared at the bottle in her hand, weighing this decision as BJ tracked the moonlight's play over her fingernails.

Maybe it *was* a bunch of doves that flew out of her head that night, BJ thought. But then again, in that darkness, those birds could've been any color at all.

The Eviction

Sex for you is loss, not love.

You lose the street sounds, you forget everything is upside down. Because all there is, is pressure, heat, the image of a tether and a fast, mean little tomcat toying with the frayed ball at the end of it. Gray fur, patchy from an existence spent under restaurant dumpsters, or too close to carpet. You cut into the woman as she cuts into you.

Afterward, you find the city again, you hear it again, through the small opening that constitutes her window. Seven stories down are brooms, beating dust from rugs into the wind tunnels. Hubcaps rolling, pushed by laughing children, tracing metallic waves into the sludge of the streets. Thudding, like broken dreams, against those rotting wooden pallets.

This is her bedroom: Small yellow stains on big white walls, mosquitoes trapped years ago in then-wet paint. Death by latex, sweeter than amber. Sunlight coursing through that slit of a window.

Yet the room is bright, which fails to explain the umbrella. There is no rhyme nor reason for an open goddamned umbrella in the middle of a sunny day in the ghetto, especially when laying *inside*, on the bed of a pretty girl whom you've known less than a week: only for things, like the veins stretched to capacity on the back of your hand, which *remind* you of umbrellas. But it is useless to try to remember to ask her why the umbrella is there, in a room where there is no rain.

You are black curves that meet again in reckless places, you are hisses like monsoon season, against these sheets. Enveloping, enfolding, and drifting into one another. She rolls her head into your neck, your sense of smell returns. Flesh, it's the scent of coming home.

And then outside, a single clap. Sarcastic ovation, the report of a government-issue .44. Your eyes and hers find the bulge in the hip pocket of your standard-issue khakis, which are hanging on the knob of the bedroom door above your metal clipboard, which is stuck halfway under the door.

Through the slit of her window you hear feet shuffling, doors shutting, you can feel the flies and gnats hush their wings and wait. Cars, heavy trucks heaving along the freeway that girdles this well-lit, eternally dark city. The creak of the first door to open rises from seven stories below.

Someone expires heavily. Then a loud bang, like the sound of a metal clipboard against the street, and another gunshot, this one aimed at the sky.

"Cooperate, people," says one masculine voice. "Just please, *please* cooperate." The fading grind of military boots on a dirty street as he shuffles away. The noise of the street returning to its proper levels.

There is perspiration and other fluids all over the both of you. You need a shower, but you won't risk it. And it bothers you a little, that the only thing you can think of now, *right* now, is that you want this woman something bad—right now and again and again. You have since the moment you met her. She makes figure eights, with a finger, in the slick on your stomach. Like she always does.

"One more time," she says, her Puerto Rican voice husky with exhaustion. "Then that's it. *Finito*. It's over."

The Driver

The limousine took Edenton to Hillsborough, glancing icy puddles in the road. Mr. Booth, who'd instructed his driver to blow that hundred on a two-dollar hot dog, was really losing it, the driver decided. The guy had been acting crazy all day. Every couple minutes this and that about how the New Year being here in five hours was all hooey, going by the original calendar used by the original church, which, Booth kept saying, is *definitely* Catholic. How the New Year happened days ago, and more bullshit about time's contradictory and arbitrary nature.

Handing The Man his dog through the divider, the driver wondered how it was to be rich and coked-up, to manage each and every day to get precisely what you want. The Man wanted to be at the coast by midnight, so that's where this rig was headed, plain and simple. He wanted only a dollar bill in change from that vendor … which got the driver to thinking how awful it would be working in this wet freeze. *He* couldn't, not for all the money in the world, not with this flu. Times Square last year, before the move, had been enough. A million people with plenty of money, and none with any common sense.

But New York was for the birds now anyways, the driver thought. A desolate place, a destructive and disappointing city. No place to raise kids or keep a decent woman anymore. He blew his nose hopelessly, considered the old days, how he didn't miss them—not the knife fights in the Bronx when he was a kid, or the quickies with junkies behind dumpsters in Chinatown, or Coney Island, or even the old, disgusting ocean. Nothing but memories, which is an infection that just won't quit ... he'd had a rabbit once, that he'd loved, in Brooklyn. It shit raisins all over the floor of the apartment before he finally had it put to sleep. *That* had been The City. A TV that worked half the time, cable that worked the other.

He tried blowing his nose again and put it all out of his mind, then handed Booth the bill, and in the rearview mirror watched his boss roll it to a practiced cylinder. Then the driver smiled and let his elbow drop and hit just the right button, and Booth's window shot down as well, and the wind rushed in and The Man grabbed for the plate in his lap, and the hot dog fell and the cocaine turned to dust in the wind. And these two men, for completely different reasons, quickly forgot that there had ever been a dollar bill inside their limo.

Phantom Power

Manuel's no-show job kept him eight to five down at Carson Cement, so it was Linda's responsibility to have the house cleaned, and dinner fixed, and the recliner angled right, and the remotes in clear sight, and Manuel's drink—a screwdriver with a mandarin/key-lime mixture made from scratch—ready for the man the moment he got home from work.

She had always kept a clean home, so that part was simple. Tidying, some picking up. A bit of careful dusting, making sure the rag she used on the borders of the flatscreen didn't leave another expensive, injurious scratch on the face of it. She had to close the curtains, too, because it was part of what he wanted, how he liked things. Dinner was potatoes, mashed or roasted with onions, olive oil, rosemary. The beans Manny liked came out of a can, but the meat—steak or chops, depending on the sale at Ray's—*had* to be cooked over charcoal, in that little grill by their back door. The recliner was simple ... or simpl*er*, ever since Linda started marking the angle he liked best with a felt-tip pen that barely showed, a mark only she could see. The remotes, too, were easy.

It was the drink that took longest and had her panicked now. They lived in an old Levittown ranch, the 50th block of Alan Avenue. It was 5:00 p.m., and through their living room window stretched the Tehachapi Mountains and wind farms to the east, the shuttered women's prison to the west. On that clear spring afternoon Linda pulled the curtains shut, thinking solely of her husband, what he liked and wanted.

Five minutes later the house was ready, dinner cooking, recliner and remotes ready to go. She went to make the drink then realized she'd forgotten to stop by Ray's on her way back from meeting Tommy at Haversack's, to pick up the oranges she *should've* picked up when she'd gone when she'd said she was going to, which was this morning. One orange left, a can of juice, a half-finished pint of lemonade: She would have to fudge the mix, and pray he'd be too high to note the difference.

By ten-past, she was squeezing the halved orange with one hand and measuring out the vodka with the other. There were key limes, at least. Linda quartered one, squeezed it into an ice-filled tumbler and added vodka, juice, mint. She finished at 5:12, two minutes late. Rather, *he* was two minutes late, and while this was abnormal, she was grateful for it.

Linda could feel the pork sizzling out back. She could smell the potatoes steaming, drying out in the oven. The house was empty and quiet and dark, and although she could not explain this sensation, she felt the danger threaded through this place, like the movement one feels in a bound-up spring. She checked the oven thrice, turned it down, reset the timer. She went out back to flip the chops and stoke the briquettes. She went back inside and straightened cushions, then drew drapes until they covered the windows perfectly, until the light outside pushed at them like air at the skin of a balloon. Twenty-past came and went, and her husband was now later than she'd ever known him to be … and the more time passed the less relieved she felt, the heavier with dread the air in that house became. At twenty-three after, she could stand it no longer. Linda went to check the mail.

Bills. An Easter card from Manuel's mother. Credit offers, which Manuel always forbade her to open, which he'd instructed her to immediately toss into the grill. She took the junk mail out back, burned it—and suddenly there it was, that feeling again. Grief, worry ... relief? Maybe, she thought, he'd had an accident. Maybe his motorcycle had been sideswiped and the bastard was facedown in the culvert by Highway 58. Maybe, just maybe, he'd still be there tonight, *late* tonight, crying out for help, mewling like a little baby girl making nothing but tiny, soundless bubbles in the mud, until she remembered that her cell was on vibrate and in her purse.

One call and a voicemail, both from Allie, Manuel's fat sister, a former prostitute who lived with her kids outside of Reno. They'd never met but Linda had seen Manuel's pictures of her, and she'd spoken with Allie by phone on the holidays. She knew Allie mostly through Manuel's complaints about her: those stories from when his sister had been addicted to *everything*. It had always bothered Linda that Allie didn't even bother driving down from Reno to the courthouse for the wedding. She'd always thought Allie hated her. This phone call was a surprise.

Linda poked at the screen of her phone and immediately heard a voice that reminded her of Manuel at his angriest ... except this voice was higher pitched, and it sounded as if Allie had run upstairs to make the call. "Linda," she said, kids screaming in the background, "Allie here. Manny's sister, he called today. Piss-drunker than I ever heard him before. I shouldn't be telling you this, but I guess I'm calling because something is up with him, and maybe you too, or maybe the both of you? He's my brother. I can smell it." And that was it.

The phone had buzzed twice in Linda's hand as she listened to the voicemail. A couple swipes and she saw the reason for it: two texts from Tommy. "He knows," read one. "RUN!" screamed the other, and Linda's vision instantly blued. She reached behind her for the wall there, felt it. Her sight began to clear, her heart began to slow. She put the phone in her pocket and began to run.

She grabbed her wallet and keys from a corduroy jacket from the living-room closet. Pall Malls and a pack of matches, shimmied into Manuel's Chico State hoodie—his favorite—then bolted out front without shutting off the grill or the oven. Five minutes later, she'd covered the two miles to Haversack's, the bar off Highway 58 where Tommy Schleeman tended Tuesday through Saturday, noon to close.

The place was a glorified doublewide on a makeshift foundation, converted over the years into something just solid enough to pass muster with the city. Linda parked her Dart down the street, around the corner from the bar's gravel lot. She grabbed her things from the passenger seat, dropped her cell into the console, and left the car running. She walked around to the rear of the bar, where Tommy parked.

His was a Monte Carlo from the early 1970s, gray with a half-rotted cloth top and a busted lock on the passenger side. Linda slid into it and felt at the bottom of the dash for the ledge where Tommy stashed his spare. The bar's jukebox was going, Miranda Lambert's "Kerosene" cranked up nice and hot: She could be crashing around in a Sherman tank out here, and no one inside would know it.

She started Tommy's car, saw the gas gauge at half ... which he'd told her, more than once, meant there was actually just a quarter-tank left. But that was enough to get her to Bakersfield. She pulled the shifter down, nudged the vehicle to the road, eased onto her side of the highway, then punched the accelerator hard as she reached for her purse and counted the money it contained.

In Bakersfield, Linda slowed, cut across to Ment Avenue, to the Chase branch there, left Tommy's ride running as she cinched her hood tight and went to the ATM. He'd always kept a firm eye on the cash, Manny did, and he wouldn't let her work, so for years Linda had tried to be frugal with whatever funds he saw fit to dole out weekly, for groceries and such. She would spend as little as possible then put the rest in an account, one she'd started the day after the wedding, her own little secret. But three years of this had netted only $200.75.

She had a debit card, but she also knew enough not to use it. He'd gone to school with half the tellers here, he would find her in a minute if she used it. So it was the ATM, even though that meant leaving those precious, hard-earned quarters behind. She added the $200 to the $31.55 already in her purse, and drove down to fill up at the Stop 'n' Sip outside of town.

Manny had never been north of San Francisco in his life. At the junction for Interstate 5, with $179 and little else in her purse, Linda made her first deliberate decision since Allie's voicemail and went north, didn't stop until she hit Sacramento and *had* to, for gas and the toilet. Filling up at the Valero there was another $55, leaving her $124 in cash.

Tommy kept a half-full bottle of Desoxyn in his dash; they were there, he'd told her late one night when Manny was off in L.A. working his *real* job, so whenever Tommy took a smoke break during a double, he could pop some to smooth out those fourteen-hour shifts. Inside the Valero, Linda spent another $4.00, this time on snacks and pop. She swallowed three Desoxyn in a single gulp then hit the highway again, due north, leaving Sacramento behind with no real idea how far those pills, or her cash, would take her.

Around 2:00 a.m., she reached Yreka. The only open place in that silent town where Linda could refuel was a truck stop, a T/A with a couple small islands for regular cars out front. The true trucker's part was out back: two rows of diesel filling stations with sixteen nozzles each, and a huge parking lot with oversized spaces where worn-out long haulers could stop and recharge.

It was a hot and sticky night, unusual for late spring that far north. Because she knew what it did to the mileage of her own car, Linda had resisted the urge to use the Monte Carlo's AC—the one accessory that Tommy had *always* made sure kept working. She'd long since dumped Manny's hoodie, and although she didn't realize this, the skintight tank top she'd been wearing all day was now fused with sweat to her body. And then she saw herself in the eyes of the trucker at the back of the store, the one screwing her with his gaze, up and down, through the open door of the beer cooler.

He was balding yet had a long, gray ponytail. He wore a black T-shirt advertising a Volvo dealership in Nevada, a brown woven-leather belt, and a silver signet ring with a bright red cross on it. He had a paunch, too, that seemed his main source of propulsion. She could hear the store's PA: "Trucking," by the Dead, and she watched this man waddle to the music as he closed the door of the cooler and began strutting like a peacock, cutting the space between them degree by degree.

And Linda let him. She weighed the $57.75 that she had just spent on gas, the $62.25 she still had left, the hunger that had been needling her since Sacramento; she thought of how hard and fast she'd been running, how she still didn't know when and where she would stop; she thought of the fact that her period would begin soon, that she'd need to buy something for it any time now, and she let that man come up to her, buy her beer, feed her, and lead her out back to his big rig, parked there like a beast asleep in a den with many other beasts. And when they were done, when he finished, she had another $100 in her pocket.

She also had a destination—*his* suggestion, the trucker's, based on a story *his* mother had told him long ago, about an aunt who'd had to get away in the 1970s and disappear, fast. She took half his case of beer with her back to Tommy's car.

Linda chewed then swallowed eight more Desoxyn at once, chased them with a lukewarm Bud, then started driving again. She stopped and did it all once more, at a Flying-J near Grants Pass: this time with a lean and brutal cuss, who banged her head into the steering wheel and ripped off a chunk of her hair before paying her $25 less than they'd originally agreed.

At eight in the morning, Linda groaned through the outskirts of Eugene and into the parking lot of a Motel 6 with rooms available at $35 a night. The clerk, a thin woman with pockmarked cheeks and teeth that looked brushed with battery acid, smiled the best she could and let Linda check in early.

Sixteen hours straight Linda slept, each hour feeling like the death of days.

*

A recovering meth addict who'd been given enough second chances to feel that she ought to pay it forward, the clerk, Sadie, held off the maids and let the sorriest, most desperate looking guest she'd ever seen sleep three hours past checkout. When Linda finally woke, cleaned up, and went to pay, Sadie covered half the balance herself and gave the poor woman one of the motel's business cards, with the name, address, and phone number of the Eugene Mission scrawled on back.

When Linda got to the mission and saw herself in the mirror behind the receptionist, she remembered the sorry way that clerk had looked at her. She looked a mess but the mission staff passed zero judgments, asked no searching questions. They seemed to pride themselves on this approach, so Linda let them.

They asked about drugs, kids, religion, whether Linda was a vegetarian or vegan, her preference for top or bottom bunk, and any issues sleeping in the dark. They asked if she needed a locker, or had a bag that needed stowing, if she was pregnant or if there were any gynecological services she might require. They showed her the chapel, the cafeteria, the beds, the barber, the laundry. Three free days, they said, then $2.00 a day, and she could earn more than that with daily chores. Chapel was required, and the woman said this was set in stone. Linda thanked them all, took another shower. She changed into the pajamas the mission provided and then slept again, for another twelve hours.

Her dreams that night weren't dreams, but recollections of what she'd recently done. She'd tossed the plates of the Monte Carlo and left the car idling out back of the motel. She then used some of the remaining money for a cab. En route to the mission, she got the cabbie to stop at the bus station, next to a trash bin where she deposited her license and Social Security and Safeway cards, anything that might be used to identify her. Deborah was who she was now, Deborah Clark, the name of the manager listed on the front of the hotel's business card.

She'd made those truckers use rubbers; even the cuss had obliged, as if he'd been burned that way before. Who she was, who she had been, was something that she'd scrubbed off in the showers at the hotel and the mission, a rank skin that shed with hard scrubbing, trailing after itself as it spiraled into the drain.

Yet the next morning, when she woke to the chime for breakfast served, Deborah threw off her sheets and blankets and began clawing at the air above her, in fierce battle with some moist and enveloping phantom power: a choking thing that she could not see, drowning her in an ooze so thick that it took a while to realize that at some point during the night, she had let herself go and wet the bed.

*

There was a man whom Deborah had heard the staff call Sunrise, and at first she'd thought it was a joke. Twice a week, each Wednesday and Saturday morning at 11:00, Sunrise would truck in beets, potatoes, squash, and whatever else was in season, from the garden that the culinary students at the community college tended to year-round. He was a roly-poly guy, about two inches shorter and a full foot wider than Deborah. When Sunrise spoke, which wasn't often, he did it so softly that even those who knew him well had to lean in to listen. And when he walked, he shambled so hesitantly, so lazily, that Deborah suspected he was constantly stoned.

It took her a couple weeks to overhear his name, another couple more to casually (and secretively) ensure that she'd heard it right, and another three to finagle a way for them to meet privately, without anyone at the mission catching on. At first, the mission's emphasis on segregating its male and female guests had made her smile. But what had felt quaint now began to seem creepy and strange: Something else in life that was being forced upon her.

Across the hall, down from the mission's pantries and coolers, was the chapel. Services took place there every night, the biggest on Saturday nights and Sunday mornings. But the space was almost always empty from 10:00 to 11:30 a.m. on Saturdays, so Deborah, thinking of Sunrise and the chapel's location near the pantry, picked that timeslot for her personal conversations with God, or whomever.

The chapel was warmly lit, wood paneling running a foot down from the ceiling, mirroring the grain of the lectern and pews. At first, since she was only there to establish the cover of routine, Deborah would bring a notebook and pass the time by drawing faces and sketching the room. Cover for both him and her; cover for the day when she would reach out to this man who made her smile even when he wasn't around, whom she could hear grunting, groaning, as he unloaded box after box, food that he gave his time to deliver for the benefit of the hopeless and the addicted, the homeless and the poor.

Four Saturdays in, something changed. *Deborah* changed, or began to change: She started leaving the notebook in her locker, sitting in the pews, thinking about life, *her* life, the one she'd left behind. She thought of Manuel, how things had begun with him, what they'd turned into, how they'd ended. She thought of God too, and fate and will and circumstance, and poor Tommy Schleeman, who used to take her up to the wind farms to watch the stars late at night when Manuel was off in L.A. working, doing to other people what she was pretty sure he'd already done to Tommy. Tommy, who loved that stupid Monte Carlo more than anything, who'd never put his hands on a woman in a hurtful way in his life.

And then she began to wonder at Sunrise: She imagined his life, what he must be like outside the mission, away from his job. This kind man who looked like the sort of hippy who would keep a garden just to watch butterflies flit and flowers grow. *They* could keep a garden, Deborah thought. *They* could find an apartment together, maybe lease a plot on the edge of town, spend next year's growing season scratching in the dirt, digging through the grime that coated them, springing into one another's arms. By her seventh Saturday morning in the chapel, Deborah realized she'd started kneeling, and could not recall when this whole kneeling thing had begun.

Eight Saturdays in, she was there on her knees, eyes shut, hands stitched together in prayer—when she heard the sound of a body rising from a pew. She opened her eyes, turned to the right … but the large circular figure with a backside like melted marshmallows was already headed back down the hall.

On the cushion next to Deborah was a small honeysuckle-scented slip the size of a nametag, on which he'd written his name and number. And at the bottom was a single word, "Namaste," in cursive, festooned with daisies, lilies, fractals, sketched and painted in inks, oils, and watercolor—

*

He said, "I've been thinking about this all day, meeting you. Talking to you. Conversing with you." And though he delivered this in a whisper, the shape of the chapel sent his plosives and sibilants twisting through space, echoing in the room's many corners and recesses.

And she said, "Oh," blushed, looked him in the eye for a moment, then looked down again, this time at the gap between them—which, since neither had moved, seemed to be shrinking on its own. *Ah*, she thought, *magnetism*. "Quiet," Deborah whispered. "Aren't you afraid?"

Earlier that morning, while cleaning the women's bathroom, Deborah had, for the first time in a week, caught a glimpse of herself in a mirror. She remembered how she used to look, before Manuel; she remembered the state she was in the day she got to the mission. At her wedding she was 5'5" and a curvy 135 pounds. Her auburn hair was long back then, down to the small of her back, with curls that flowed into one another like waves of light or communication.

She had bright blue eyes and fair skin, and freckles that migrated with each change in the angle of the sun. Toni, her bestie in Tehachapi, had wanted to conceal them the day of the wedding, but Linda had said no: Everyone who saw the pictures said those freckles added depth to who she was.

By the time she got to the mission, Linda had dropped 15 pounds in two days. The skin on her face was loose, and there were bruises on her neck and arms, some so deep they seemed implanted far beneath the surface of her skin. Her nails broken, her lips cracked and dry: She'd left a patch of that long auburn hair in the passenger side of a Continental long-hauler in Grants Pass.

But in the months since, Deborah had gained all the weight back and then some, the extra pounds a happy fat evenly dividing itself between her working bits. She looked curvy again, and though she tried to cover it up, she got the occasional disapproving look from the female staffers. She'd always been proud of her shape. She could try to hide that from men, but never from women.

When the bruises faded, Deborah went to the barber at the mission, a Mexican named Paolo who was training to be a stylist at the cosmetology school three blocks away. He gave her a cute bob, shortest cut of her adult life, and she quickly got into the habit of tucking it behind her ears, so the back of her head was always where she carried it most.

Deborah's lips healed quickly. About a month into her stay, Sherry, one of the mission's youngest staffers—a college student who'd gotten a DUI and started working there as community service—gave Deborah a brand-new tube in a shade of pink that said the young girl had a good eye ... and Deborah, in turn, treasured the lipstick and used it sparingly. Since receiving his note, each Saturday morning before chapel, she'd pull out the lipstick and apply a bit of it at a time, daubing her lips with tissue until her lips alone seemed responsible for her renewed and resonant glow. She'd arch her back then, push out her breasts and backside then, deciding once again that she was starting to like what she saw.

So when she asked the man if he was afraid, and he moved even closer, close enough that she could feel his breathing, the warmth of his body radiating in tangible waves—when he put his hand on hers and she snapped her head toward him and looked at his face, she *knew*. Even before he replied to her question, she *knew*.

"No way," he answered. "I'm not afraid. Not even the tiniest little bit. Are you?"

*

That winter was colder, grayer, wetter than ever, and Deborah, who'd never before spent a winter in the Pacific Northwest, did all she could to make it through. She read as many books as she could afford to buy, from the dollar bin at the downtown Smith Family. She snagged a beat-up acoustic in the lost and found at the mission, then sat about humming and strumming, picking up whatever she could from any of the few dozen of the mission's guests who played guitar, and string-by-string, chord-by-chord, Deborah began to learn how to play. When she and Sunrise got together, they went for walks in the rain, or picnicked in waterlogged forests, or sat for hours chatting in sodden parks and the fields near the buttes. He had an umbrella so large it shielded them together from the drops of rain that often fell but sometimes swirled up, from the wintery clouds that shielded the entire western part of the state: from the rays of the moon, the stars. Even, eventually, the sun.

They were dating. She developed a new gait, as if something dense had shifted from her shoulders, or simply fallen on its own and shattered in a million pieces on the mission floor. No one but the two involved knew the reason for it, but *everyone* noticed the change. Each Saturday after they first spoke, he would drop off another ornate note and disappear before anyone could see. And each Saturday evening they would meet a few blocks away, near the downtown library, and do whatever it was he'd promised earlier on his note.

His given name was indeed Sunrise, Sunrise Zimmerman, and he'd lived in Eugene all his life. His parents, both dead, two hippies who'd met at Haight-Ashbury in the 1960s and stayed through its wild decline, had moved to Eugene in the early 1980s, shortly before his birth. He was shy, introspective, but spoke louder and more freely with her than she'd ever seen him do with anyone else— and she in turn expressed herself with him like she hadn't with anyone in years, not Toni, not Tommy, and *definitely* not Manuel. She told him her real name was Lucinda Bunting, that she'd left her hometown of Yreka with nothing, running from an ex who'd liked to rip out her hair and bang her head into the steering wheel ... and then she told him the truth about Manny and his *real* job, the contracts he carried out at night sometimes for the cartels in L.A. She said that she could never go back, and Sunrise comforted and caressed her as she spoke, accepting everything she told him without judgment.

He was a computer geek, and what he didn't know how to do, his cadre of fellow geeks, some local and some not, could readily accomplish. It was Sunrise, with the help of friends Alex and Matt (ApophisL7 and 3asygr3asy, respectively), who turned "Linda Starling" into "Deborah Clark," at least in the eyes of the government. By midwinter she had a birth certificate, a license, a passport, and a Social Security card, all brand new and bona fide, with her new name on them. Shortly afterward, in February, Deborah left the mission and moved in with Sunrise.

He lived off a feeder that led from the southbound side of the interstate to the community college about a half-mile down. His house was a cozy, fully carpeted three-bedroom with cream-colored siding. Sunrise was a "patient" (migraines): One of the bedrooms had fluorescent lights everywhere and functioned as a nursery, while the finished attic was bisected by black plastic sheeting, with lights and buckets of water and nutrients for growing indoors during winter. There was a big, well-tended backyard, too, with high fences along which he'd set up discreet plots for growing when the outdoor season came. It took a while but Deborah began to think of it as medicine, even to welcome the haze that often hung upon him. She came to associate the scent of weed with coming home.

It took them three weeks to clear the adjustment period that most couples spend several months or even a year getting through. She learned that he *liked* to dust and vacuum, that he enjoyed doing his own laundry and folding his own clothes: that he liked making breakfast but enjoyed it when she made lunch. And he preferred beer, *not* cocktails. She taught him much about herself, too: how it was a bad idea to let her start complaining, since sometimes she didn't know when or how to stop; the degree to which she hated cleaning the bathroom, especially the tub and toilet, after a man; the way she liked being woken up for sex in the middle of the night, and how little she enjoyed being frisky first thing in the morning.

The first time they'd slept together was two weeks after his first note, but he'd never let her go down on him or get a good look at his private parts until *after* she'd moved in ... and when he did, she understood why: He'd had a partial orchiectomy in his teens, after being diagnosed with testicular cancer, and while he explained this meant he couldn't have kids, he'd been lucky enough to be spared some of the other effects. He told her this … and she looked at the scar, touched him there, wondered silently how much lower his testosterone must be because of it. Then she grabbed his head and kissed him, said that she loved him, all of him, every present and missing part. Promised him she'd do so forever.

They married that summer, mid-August. At the Eugene Rose Garden: Smallish ceremony, peopled with mission staffers and current *and* former residents, ministered by Trillium Starchild, a longtime friend of Sunrise's who'd become a minister online for the occasion.

Wearing a druid robe and silver rings on each finger, Trillium Starchild did an excellent job with a ceremony that both bride and groom knew was illegal.

*

She gave them everything they asked for: ID in the form of a driver's license, symptoms, history, all forms filled out in block letters to the best of her knowledge and ability. She had no job but Sunrise did, so she was covered insurance-wise. She did what they said, went to the desk when called, waited as long as they deemed necessary. When the women up front finally beckoned, and the one in charge walked her back, Linda smiled as if the elegantly coiffed physician's assistant next to her, the one getting paid and not doing the paying, was doing the whole world, especially Linda, the biggest of favors.

They took vitals. They measured her up and down and side to side, asked question after humiliating question, and she calmly and repeatedly relayed the difficult and graphic answers: no to the discharge, yes to the burning and tingling—a small spot like a welt from a tiny whip on the bottom-left flap of her labia … and yes, she answered: yes, it was fucking *painful.*

He was a balding man whose patience and directness spoke to years of experience and levelheaded practice. She removed her skirt and underwear; he took a brief look and told her what he thought it looked like, what she'd thought it was in the first place. The doctor then explained what would happen next: the blood test and, if it came back with the result they suspected, the phone call from the Oregon Department of Human Services, who would register her as a carrier and request phone numbers of all recent partners. The doctor, as he recited this, was inhumanly calm, and Linda's eyes drifted up to his pate, where she imagined the deep gray luminescence of a rainy winter's day, and not the fluorescents hovering above them in the windowless room, as responsible for the gleam she saw there.

Eyes shut, she imagined the rain drizzling on the street outside, spiking the surface of the millrace like grains of sand sprinkled from the heavens. She convinced herself that those weren't raindrops but tears, ones *she'd* supplied—that there were actual tears falling from her eyes, streaming down her face and falling into the millrace, though she'd never known a time in her adult life when she'd been able to cry. She'd actually begun pushing at her tear ducts, heaving herself at whatever it was that was blocking them, wondering whether it was the smell of the office, the strawberry scent of disinfectant, that was responsible for her current inability to weep, for this delay in desired and richly deserved weeping—when she felt the warmth of the doctor's hand upon her own.

"Wait here," he said. "The nurse will return in a moment and draw your blood. We'll call you in three days with the lab results. Deborah," he said, looking at her ring, "you said you're married?"

"Yes, recently."

"Yes, and you don't think you got this from him?"

"No," she said, thinking of Sunrise, his limited sexual history. "Probably not," she said slowly, as if listening to herself saying it.

The doctor squeezed her hand: "Any reason for us to worry after your safety? Because he *has* to be informed. But there are many, many different ways—"

"No. My husband would *never* touch me, nothing like that. Please," she said, jerking her hand out from under his.

He grew tall and rigid, brushing at the pressed thighs of his trousers. He spun on his heels to the door, repeating that the nurse would be in shortly as he walked out. Linda left the clinic before anyone had the chance to draw her blood. She then took a bus downtown, where Sunrise was finalizing an afternoon delivery to a university co-op.

*

That night, she made his favorite meal: plank-grilled salmon with a wasabi-soy sauce, ginger-sugar marinade; risotto with portobello mushrooms; greens with sliced strawberries, grape tomatoes, drizzled with sweet balsamic vinaigrette. The risotto she made in two batches: one with regular butter, and one with enough of his medicated olive oil to make the dish potent without noticeably altering the taste.

For the forty-five minutes it took to cook the salmon, Linda stood under an umbrella in the rain, manipulating the temperature and ports of the grill while Sunrise worked upstairs on his most recent crop. Eight plants were flowering on the far side of the sheeting; she could smell them from where she stood out back, a good ten yards from the house. A deep and verdant scent. It surprised her to realize how much she would miss it.

They had a bottle of wine with dinner, a bright char- donnay from a vintner Sunrise went to high school with, whose winery was somewhere out in Veneta. She would miss this too, the gently bragging, name-dropping part of him. They ate, they drank, they were happy together. They made love, twice, no protection.

The wine and sex together amplified his risotto: By 8:30 that evening, Sunrise was out cold, with one fat white leg sticking out from under the covers. When he started snoring, Linda rose, got dressed, grabbed some essentials from the dresser and closet and bathroom, threw them all into a duffel bag, and left the bedroom without once looking back at him.

She took his keys and his wallet, threw her stuff in the passenger seat of his van, and then went back into the house, to the cabinet under the sink in the laundry room. She took out the jumbo-sized bottle of bleach there and poured a cup into the soil of each and every plant in the house, the ones that were flowering, the ones in the veg- etative state, even the clones isolated downstairs, in the extra room. When she finished that, Linda drove to the bank and withdrew $400 from his checking account. She then returned to the house, dropped his wallet into the mail slot, hit I-5 south, and flicked on the cruise control. She took her time this go-round, yet didn't dawdle: What had taken her thirteen hours nearly two years ago now took her twenty-four.

*

At ten that night came a banging on his front door and Manuel leapt out of his recliner, scrambled down the hall, grabbed the .30-06 from the closet, and shimmied, his back to the wall, into his living room. He'd passed out early, his heart was still racing from a horrifying dream: Something, some invisible power, chasing him through a shopping mall, and whatever it was had just cornered him in the women's bathroom at Macy's. Manny shouldered the door open thinking only of his dream, the stupid mistake he'd made in it, and how he wouldn't be making it now. He almost shot the woman in the face when he realized who it was.

Linda walked into his house like she owned it. But it was Deborah who waved Manny's gun aside, shutting the door quickly behind her.

I Love You, Joe

I mean I guess it all started that day at Jefferson Cole, which calls itself a high school even though it's really just three two-story cellblocks, triangles painted yellow with brown hallways and white lockers, and thick green glass with black wire crossed up inside. There's smaller buildings, too, like the cafeteria, that you had to go outside to get to … but even those, with bars over the windows instead of the chicken wire in the glass, have the same low-down, locked-up, and locked-in feel of this place. Halfway through the first day of school and here I was getting kicked out of history class for, of all things, calling a thing by its proper name. I could smell the caf, the deep fryer getting ready for lunch, the moment I left the room and stepped into the hallway.

The school's offices were bottom center, a glassed-off suite behind a gurgly fountain and some tired-looking plastic trees. I woke the secretary there, tickling her nose with the note my history teacher, Mr. Westerburg, wrote up on me. The way that lady, with her puffed-up hair and serious face and huge pink glasses, jumped up and stamped the note … She pointed the way and buzzed the door, mad as hell.

I remember marching into the principal's office, which was an office with wooden stuff and a kind of heavy silence, and yellow lights. The principal was a principal, sitting behind a desk with a black phone shaped like a Bible on it. The back corner of the room was basically this wooden planter-thing with one fat dead cactus inside and I remember thinking: How do you kill a cactus? I mean seriously, how *do* you kill a cactus?

I walked in and the man didn't move. He didn't say anything, not until I fell into a chair and said what I was there for: telling Mr. Westerburg what my father Joe had always told me, that it was the Battle of Bull Run, and only disappointed rednecks still called it the Battle of Manassas. Which is when this guy, this high school *principal*, shot up and yelled for me to get the hell out of his office and stop wasting his time with this crap … which I did. I grabbed my bag and shut his door right as the lunch bell rang, and I jogged over to the caf and sat alone, in a corner by a window with meatloaf that was soggy and yet smelled deep-fried. Even the milk was a day from the date on the carton. But like my pops used to say, people in Africa are starving. So I ate.

J. Cole's caf was like our caf: busy and noisy, with a lot of look-alike people dressed in the same-type clothes, all eating the same-type food: The End. After that was gym and then French, which I was only taking because I already knew it. Then Honor's English and our teacher, Ms. Andrews, a small white lady with a big butt and horn-rims and short, brown curls. At the beginning of class, she announced that she'd decided over summer that not only were we going to kick off the year with Shakespeare, we'd also be reading *Hamlet* first, for fuck's sake.

The other kids in the class … it was like every other AP class I'd ever taken. All white, and mostly girls. The girls, they started taking turns interrupting each other with how they liked Hamlet the guy, and they'd seen the movie as a kid, and my-oh-my hadn't such-and-such looked so-and-so with a goddamned sword. I just kept thinking about how I'd read that stupid thing four times already, only once because I'd wanted to, and anyways got bored silly with that stupid movie by the middle. But they kept on talking, so I pulled one of my father's sci-fi anthologies out of my bag.

My father, he loved sci-fi. Last time I saw him, it was early morning and he was in his bathroom reading some story or another while brushing his teeth. Not a care in the world that morning, not one single hint on his face that late that evening while I was studying down the street at my friend's place, he'd leave the house, start the car, and never come back. He had this regimen where, each morning while scanning some book, he would brush and floss and run this sleek gizmo in his mouth, then use those pink pills to see if he got all the plaque ... and then he'd do the whole thing all over again if the pink stuck to his teeth.

It happened a lot, that he would catch me looking in and he'd do this bit where he would aim the thing at me, push the button, and laugh until froth spattered and dribbled down his chest. I always thought it was hilarious ... but looking back now, maybe it wasn't so funny. It got worse, though, during the big strike: He started cleaning his mouth that way five times a day, as if trying to fill up all the extra time the bosses and union leaders made sure he'd had.

Anyway, I'd been working my way through his Nebula Award collections all summer long, the ones from '70 to '73. Those were the only ones I had, the ones he'd left behind in the storage room in Detroit when he left me and my mom. I was about halfway finished with '73, the last one left, in the middle of this story about a little girl who was five hundred years old, on account of this potion she had that, if she took it every century or so, kept her young.

Her history teacher, he was talking about the Industrial Revolution. And *she* was putting it to *him* because he was saying all of this boneheaded stuff about child labor. I liked that, how she was putting it to him, and she was just getting sent to *her* principal's office for correcting *her* teacher when suddenly there it was: Ms. Andrew's hand, spread like a fan across the page of my book.

Everything got quiet as I looked up. She was grinning her grin, Ms. Andrews, a little forced one that was tight and wide and straight. I thought of how I hadn't even tried to hide the book ... but I hadn't figured I needed to either, not in *English* class. So I yanked it out from under her hand, put it in my bag with my notebook and pen. I zipped the whole thing up. She waited until I got to the door before saying anything.

Ms. Andrews said my name like she was asking a question, and it didn't stop there, like it ever does. "Mind telling me where the heck you think you're going?" she asked, and I thought: Is that really a question too?

"Ma'am? To the principal's office, Ma'am." And I marched on out.

Teachers. It's like what they say is never quite what they mean. She hadn't told me to sit down ... but she hadn't said go either. On the way down, I kept thinking how different things were here, how not one of the kids I'd ever seen get into trouble back home ever waited to be told to go to the office: They just went. And then the big bell rang, and all the kids came out and headed for their lockers and the streets, the bushes, and the parking lots. Everyone was there and then they weren't, they'd spread out and left.

I got to the front door and three blond kids in brown-and-yellow jerseys bumped into me ... and they weren't smiling. But this was a good thing, I remember thinking. Back in Detroit, kids like this, they said the word aloud, not with their little eyes. This way was different, so much less embarrassing. And I was suddenly glad: Glad that I wasn't in Detroit anymore, glad that everything in my life was so much better and so goddamned different. I walked the two dusty miles home and locked myself in.

I was still getting used to our new house ... not that it was actually new, not that there was a hell of a lot to get used to. Problem was, there really *wasn't* much house to get used to. It was down the street from these railroad tracks, just a small ranch-style place with red bricks and cream-colored siding. The kind of house that feels like someone built it just because they had to. Everything about it was smaller than our three-story place back in Detroit: kitchen, living room, even the bathroom. I mean it didn't even have a den.

But my mom was trying, and I knew it. She had grabbed what she could find that was cheap and as close to her parents as possible, and when I thought about it that way, it wasn't so bad. The kitchen had linoleum that from the many different greens looked left over from before I was born. Cabinets that needed staining, set far up and peeling in spots. Appliances that were solid and working and rusted out but only at the bottom, so you had to kneel and use a flashlight to tell.

It had a living room about the size of my bedroom, which wasn't saying much, with this light tan carpeting that you can find in any square mile of the continental U.S., if you put your mind to it. But like I said, it wasn't so bad. The bedrooms and the hallway, which had the same dark-brown carpeting, were lined with wood paneling that had bulges everywhere, like there was air back there pushing through the walls, trying hard to get in.

So, bad but not bad, not really. Not *bad* ... just not what I'd gotten used to my entire life. Everything we'd owned had always been new in Detroit, and I mean *everything*: house, cars, clothes, TVs, the stereo. I remember, when we first moved down, Mom didn't even have a car. She had to take the bus around, and the schedule was so messed up that it took her almost two hours each way to and from Womack, the hospital where she worked.

That night, I'd already gone to bed when I heard our front door open. A few minutes later and I could feel soft light spilling from the hallway and into my room ... which was OK since I wasn't asleep yet, not really. It wasn't midnight yet, and I hadn't been able to fall asleep before midnight in the weeks since we'd left Detroit. Anyway, Mom walked in and sat right next to me, and she sighed and began stroking my head, running her nails lightly over my scalp and calling me her sweet baby.

For a minute she didn't say much else. Which was fine with me because it always made me feel so good. We'd always been pretty tight, Mom and me, and she used to do that bit a lot when I was a little kid. Like a game, my mother would stroke my head while I pretended I was asleep. I mean, it always makes you feel good when you're somebody's sweet baby, I don't care how jaded you are. But she'd been coming in late at night and doing it more than ever lately, like something about it was making *her* feel better. So I let it happen, like always, and I kept on pretending that I was asleep.

And I breathed in deeply, like I *was* asleep. She still had that dirty, antiseptic smell that you can count on a day in a hospital and a ride on a bus to give you. She stroked my head and I sort of pushed my head into her thigh, eyes still shut, and then she stopped and got quiet, like she'd closed her eyes, too.

"Baby," Mom said, her voice even softer than normal, … almost as if she'd been crying the whole way home, which ticked me off. I mean she hadn't been crying nearly as much since we'd packed up and left Detroit. "Sometimes," she continued, "I wish I could explain.

"I wish I could explain how every day is the same thing, and that's what it means to grow up. To be *grown* up. You keep telling yourself it's what you want, that this thing, this life, is what you *need* to do. So after a while, you get to believing it. You get to expecting it. What I mean is, I'm starting to understand it, what your father did. I don't agree with it, not even a little. But at least now I'm starting to understand it."

And then my mother stopped talking. She stopped stroking my head, too, and it got so still in my room that I started to imagine that I could actually *feel* her trying to smile. "It makes me crazy sometimes," she said finally. "Everything does, except the fact that I know I've got you to come home to."

You've got to understand, my mom has the softest voice you've ever heard, hands down. More than mom-soft even. And she's got the nicest smile you'll ever see, nicer than anyone here. Pretty much born to be a nurse. But that night it was something else, something harder than normal in her voice, more than just her being tired. She started stroking my head again, and I kept on pretending that I was asleep until I *was* asleep, until I felt my left leg jerking my whole body awake.

I opened my eyes, I saw the back of my mother's robe ease between her legs, I felt the draft she made when she shut my bedroom door. Pretty soon she was behind me, under the covers, one arm over me squeezed tight, though not so tight that I couldn't breathe. And I waited until she relaxed, until my mom's own breathing got heavy and deep, before I let myself drift off into a nightmare about decaying teeth, and what happens the moment that your mother stops loving you.

*

I woke up the next day in a totally different mood. I went to school early, straight to the guidance office, to the only rack of materials there that was illuminated. Yellow bulbs in a black track in a white ceiling, all aimed at one massive rack which took up a whole wall and had row after row after row of all the stuff you'd ever need to apply to college. There were print applications to all the in-state schools; the rest of them you could use the computer or this standardized form to send off for.

I stood quietly in that room, in front of that rack and for a long time. Feeling pretty small, just trying to put together what I'd need. I mean I'd gotten a pretty good score on the PSAT that my father had made me take in Detroit, but with the strike and everything, here it was beginning of junior year and Mom and I hadn't even talked about the idea of college.

After what happened last night, though, Mom and the dream and everything … well it somehow all seemed final then, like the right thing, the *only* thing for me to do was to man up and go to college and become a dentist.

I figured both our lives would be pretty good then, if I became a dentist. I mean I could make more than enough for the *both* of us, if I went to college and became a dentist.

I grabbed one of those generic app request forms, a brochure explaining financial aid, and an application to Duke ... mostly because I'd seen them on TV back home in Detroit. Grant Hill was like a god back home in Detroit: When I was a kid, Pops would have his buddies from the plant over to watch Hill's old team play on TV and I could remember those commercials, with that white coach talking up the school, bragging on how it had one of the best pre-med programs in the country. I had the grades for it too, and if the SATs were anything like that prep test, then I knew I could make the test scores for it. I started to read the application ... and then I felt this cold, bony pressure on my shoulder.

A guidance counselor, touching me without asking. Curved-in and yellowed teeth, and a pink horizontal face. He was leaning in and looking at me in that sad and needful way, the way they always do, and I usually didn't mind it. I mean as a kid, you meet grown-ups all the time who lean forward and look like snakes, and behind that bull-shit talk of theirs, you can tell right away what they really want.

Everybody does. Everybody knows. It's like you're a person ... but you're not. Just a function, just some dear thing, just a path from where they are to where they always want to be ... and all the while somebody who's supposed to know better is trying like the devil to chip little bits off you. I mean eventually you learn that's lots of people, that there's *lots* of sick pups when it comes to kids ... but guidance counselors? Man, they want the biggest bit, *and* they want it for free.

I shook off his hand, I stood there in the silence of the room and gave the guy my hardest look, which probably wasn't all that hard, even if I had taken off my glasses. Then I snarled at him ... which probably didn't work too hot, given my braces. But I did my best and it must've worked some because he straightened up quickly, jerking his shoulders and his head, adding the extra height to his many advantages.

He had a class ring from decades before, saying UCLA where a wedding band should've been. I wanted to laugh out loud and in his face, but we just sort of looked at each other for a while, two fighters in a silent whirlwind and zero space between us.

After a while, my guidance counselor grinned. "Be realistic, son," he said, pointing to the application in my hand before patting me on the head and walking away.

It took a minute but I finally found a pen, filled out one generic application request form for UCLA, then dropped it in the bin for outgoing requests. I spent the next two weeks easing into things. I mean I figured it wasn't so bad. On the third day of school, our principal called me into his office and said that he didn't give a squat where I'd come from or what my grades or test scores were, he wouldn't be putting up with any stupid shit like what I'd pulled in Ms. Andrews' class on the first day of school, and that this was my first and final warning. I thanked him for his candor and jogged back to class.

I even read *Hamlet* again, for good measure. I just wanted to see Ms. Andrews' face when she handed back the best paper in the class with an "A+" across the top of it in angry red ink, no corrections at all. Which happened and it was priceless. We started on Socrates right after that ... and I stayed totally quiet and attentive in my little corner of the room, all the while wondering, for the umpteenth time, if it bothered *anybody at all* that all this corny ancient bullshit really was, was these dirty old dudes theorizing on why they liked slipping it to their country's best, most promising young boys.

Mr. Westerburg warmed up to me, and I cut him some slack. It was like he'd never be anything more than a shallow and offensive history teacher, and I figured what the hell can you do, he's a teacher and the guy's harmless, and besides, it was kind of funny the way he grew on you. I kept attacking his opinions and he kept on giving me A+'s mostly because he didn't know what else to do and, deep down, we sort of respected each other. Pretty soon we were eating lunch together, in the teachers' part of the caf. He really liked the idea of me trying to surprise my mom by getting into college, so he promised to write me a letter and then got Ms. Andrews and my French teacher to promise letters too, for both Duke and UCLA. The man even helped me fudge fee waiver forms, so I wouldn't have to ruin the surprise by asking Mom for money.

French was a breeze, and so was gym class. And because Mr. Westerburg told me I would need something like it to get into college, I started thinking about tennis. It was only fall; Pops had left his fancy racket behind, and Mom had played in college. It didn't take much to get her to promise to teach me enough by spring to work my way up the seeding on the JCHS varsity team.

My mother missed my father. I could tell that even if she didn't talk about it, and I knew she liked me playing tennis with her, even if I wasn't nearly as good as he was. And it gave us something to do together on the weekends, aside from me plucking out her gray, or helping her with the more physically demanding chores around the house.

At school, everyone seemed to be splitting off into groups, but I wasn't making any friends at all ... which was a relief. No one to slow me down.

One night during the fifth week of school, I saw a news story about the GM strike on the TV set ... which, thank God, came on before Mom got home from work. It was all over, the newscasters said. Stupid voices on top of foolish pictures, tired-looking workers with hands in victory signs, a lot of dumb, empty space between their fingers. It was all over. Everybody was so goddamned happy. The more I watched, the less sure I was of how she'd take it, hearing about it all again. Wondering if Pops ever showed back up for his supervisory position at the plant. So I stopped paying attention and forgot all about it and never told her.

And I decided to quit reading sci-fi and remembering my father just to keep the memory fresh ... and that, I thought, was that. All the rest of the stories in that '73 issue sucked next to the one about the little girl anyway, especially the endings. The way she skipped into the theater alone made me remember when I was a kid: How I'd pedal my own feet in the air when my parents would lift me by the arms, so we could cross the streets of downtown Detroit. It would be hard to forget him, it would be hard to let him go ... but the truth was, he had forgotten us.

So that was that: The End. No more stories, no more Pops. No more Joe.

*

Finally, Thanksgiving. Mom had just spent all her spare cash on a car, this Brougham that was about ten years old but would maybe last another couple more if she was careful with it. For Thanksgiving dinner, we went to the only family we could afford to visit: Mom's parents, who live in Haymount, this snooty little part of Fayetteville that likes to pretend it's in a whole nother town even though it clearly isn't.

I hate everything about Haymount. I hate how upscale it thinks it is, how old the houses are. I mean just because paint's peeling off some old house doesn't mean it automatically has character. Mom's folks live all alone on a hill in one of the biggest houses in the neighborhood, more than big enough for me and my mother and Hamlet and Ophelia and a whole lot of queens and ghost kings to fit into. A big and dirty white thing with wings, a huge hill of a yard, five cement birdbaths and an arched cobblestone driveway that goes round and round. I wouldn't have wanted to live there, not in a million years, not even if they *had* invited us. Anyway, we'd been there for dinner once before, when we'd first got to Fayetteville, the night they decided to gang up on Mom and I lost it.

I've never liked my mom's parents. They made a whole lot of money buying and selling crap when they were younger, so they're pretty rich, but that's not why I've always hated them. My mother's mother has this way of looking down at you even if you're taller than she is, even if you're standing on top of Mount Sinai looking down, she'll find some way of making you *feel* small: this skinny, ashy old bird with her thin, creepy voice and big dents all over her face and arms, who just keeps on finding ways to judge you all over the place. And her husband, who's old and bald and heavy, with skin the color of kitchen cabinets, and a bad habit of asking how you're doing, and then when you say, "Fine, and you?" like normal people do, he'll start telling you how he's actually doing, and I mean in *detail*. Plus, anything she says, you *know* he'll follow along with.

So, that first week: Right when we'd just moved to town, and we're sitting in their den, this plush room with dark paintings of dogs playing poker on the walls and a small gas fireplace going, and old yellow furniture covered in thick plastic. When all of a sudden I realize Grandma and Grandpa Chapman are working the conversation around in order to blame my mother for Pops freaking out during the GM strike, leaving the two of us to fend for ourselves.

First, Grandma starts in with "Heard from Joe?" All offhand, like it's the most innocent question in the world. Then Grandpa Chapman starts in too, with "Hope Joe hasn't found another one by now, maybe started another family?" Stuff like that, bouncing turns off each other like it was a goddamned tennis match and my mother was the ball: Oh, I was *fuming*. I was ready to *explode*. I was getting so hot I could feel the plastic from the sofa melting on my legs through my good goddamned best set of church pants.

And I kept thinking, one more comment. Just one more and I'm gonna have to march over to that fireplace, grab that poker, and make these two idiots feel the hell that she'd gone through. But instead of that, I thought of something smart to say and when they let off, I asked Grandma Chapman when the last time was that she'd worked an eight-hour day ... and boy did the old girl lose it. I mean she *really* lost it. Threw a HUGE fit about how when she was young, Lord have Mercy! She *never* talked out of place, blah blah blah blah *blah* ... and then Mom didn't say a word to me all the way home and for a couple days after.

So this time I sat with my mouth shut around their totally white-bread Thanksgiving spread, and I let the grown-ups have their grown-up conversation. I didn't even flinch when Grandma Chapman gave thanks for, among many other empty-headed and stupid things, "His blessed grace" in the end of the GM strike in Detroit.

Mom must've put away a half bottle of Grandma Chapman's vodka that night. I don't think her parents even noticed, seeing as they were paying so much attention to me, wondering if I would say something smart this time around. But *I* did, *I* noticed. She didn't stumble once on the way out, or even as we climbed down that cobble-stone driveway, but when we reached the car, which was parked at the bottom of the hill where no one could see, I slipped the keys from her hand and said:

"I'll drive home, Mom. OK?"

She gave me this goofy grin I'd never seen before, and then she went around to the other side of the car. Some-where in the fifteen minutes it took to get home, she fell asleep facing me, her neck arched with the curve of the head rest, her mouth slightly open like one of those CPR dolls in the nurse's office at school. I had to carry her inside but I didn't mind because it was always fun to take care of my mother. It took me ten whole minutes but I did it, laying all that dead weight under the covers of her bed and arranging her pillow so her neck wouldn't get sore by morning. She opened her eyes once and pecked me on the lips; I smoothed her hair, and then I whispered something I'd learned in school: "*Fais de beaux rêves*," I said, with all my heart, because I truly meant it. And I fixed the pillow again around my mother's neck.

It was only seven o'clock, and we didn't have any cof-fee, so I decided to take the Brougham up to this sports pub across the railroad tracks and down the street from our house, to see if they'd serve me a cuppa joe and let me read a paper. The way there I kept thinking about how little it had bothered me tonight, seeing my mother drunk for the very first time.

Well, that's not true exactly … it did and it didn't. I understood why, but it didn't make me feel disappointed or anything. It just wasn't necessary, that's all. I mean Pops, he was *history*. He was *gone*, he'd *left* us. Mom had been so strong, she'd made it so we didn't need anything outside the two of us. It just wasn't necessary, that's all, her getting that way. And if that was her reaction now, what would happen once I left for college?

Maybe, I thought, it was me. Maybe the way I *had* been just wasn't enough. Maybe things would improve if I started getting better at tennis or something, or maybe when she read an acceptance letter from UCLA—or, even better, Duke? But right then I heard a horn, saw some flashing lights, and realized not only was I sitting in a stopped car, but I'd stopped the car right on the goddamned railroad tracks of all places. It was unbelievable. I couldn't believe it. I hit the gas, skidded around the safety arm on the other side of the tracks, parked at the sports pub, and forgot all about it.

I walked into the pub and man was it the most depressing thing I'd ever seen. I got my coffee and newspaper without any funny looks from a waiter who served me and disappeared. There were muted televisions all over the place with this movie where this guy was getting shot in the back by someone you couldn't see while he was taking a piss in a bathroom at some strip joint.

The movie was muted because the jukebox was going, playing that Bob Dylan song about the Rolling Stones way too loud considering there were probably ten people in the whole spot, counting the bartender and her boy-friend. They were sitting in a corner of the rectangle that the actual bar made, and she kept taking swigs when she thought no one was watching. There was this guy sitting alone on one side of the bar with a short glass in front of him, talking out loud to no one at all.

At this table way in the back, not too far from the bartender and her boyfriend, was a blonde with this neon-green miniskirt that was hiked up where anybody who walked in the door could see the run in the crotch of her stockings. She had a shot glass in one hand, kept on rubbing her forehead with the palm of the other. I started reminding myself that it was Thanksgiving to make my-self feel better ... but then I thought about how it was *Thanksgiving*, and I was at some sports pub, getting ready to drink coffee and read the paper because my mother was at home passed out drunk, as a result of her parents blam-ing her for my father abandoning us.

I'd been drinking coffee and reading maybe fifteen minutes before I noticed Mr. Westerburg, three booths down and sitting mostly with his back to me. He was slouched across the table, swirling a yellow drink in his glass. He didn't look too good, and I decided to go over there and talk to him. Mr. Westerburg really wasn't that bad of a guy, and it was Thanksgiving, and he looked really down, so I went over and tapped him on the shoulder.

Mr. Westerburg looked up at me. He squinted and said: "Know what I used to be before I started teaching, Timmy? A priest. A goddamned alcoholic boozehound priest. I wasn't always a teacher. Nope. I used to be a priest."

He said that to me in this scratchy, burned-out voice, and his face was red and he smelled like scotch, and I could see spots all over his shirt where he'd dribbled stuff on it. I don't remember what the hell I was thinking when I sat down—maybe that I wasn't depressed enough as it was?—but I did, I sat down in the other side of the booth, and I asked the man if he'd just gotten done eating dinner with his family.

"Family," he laughed, then lit a cigarette. "I was just getting around to family. That's why I quit and became a teacher. To get married and get around to family so I wouldn't be so goddamn lonely all the time, since my parents are dead. See, they only had me," he said, closing an eye and pointing with his glass at the bartender, who left her boyfriend in the corner to get Mr. Westerburg another drink. Not that he needed one—man was my teacher *sloshed*. "I quit," Mr. Westerburg said, "to marry this bitch who used to say … you know what she used to say?"

I told him I didn't.

"She used to say, 'You can't be cool and be Christian.' You like that shit, kid? 'You can't be cool and be Christian.' Then she divorced me. Guess I wasn't cool enough, right?"

"I'm sorry, Mr. Westerburg."

"Oh, don't be," he said. "Happened a year ago. Ancient history. Taught me that one person cannot possibly give you everything that you need, or everything that you want. Wanna be a dentist, kid? Huh? You're still so young, so determined. Seven-fucking-teen. You think nothing can stand in your way? You wait. You'll get into college, you know that, right? Can see it now, with my good eye. Ten years down, big sign out front. 'Timothy Jones, D.D.S.' But none of it will matter, because nothing ever matters.

Nothing ever will. Do you think I'm a good teacher?" my teacher asked, taking a drag.

"Sure," I said. "You're the greatest."

"Think so?"

"Yeah. I mean, you're the only one I can talk to."

"Really?" His eyes were starting to light up.

"Yeah. And you're helping me with all this college stuff. I'd say you're pretty dedicated. I mean, if anybody was to ask me, I'd say you're a pretty dedicated—"

"All you ever want," Mr. Westerburg said, "is to feel like you have done *something*." He was getting misty-eyed now, and I was starting to understand how dumb I'd really been. I mean I could've just walked out without coming over, he was so drunk that he would've never noticed me, and I wouldn't have had to stand there feeling so embarrassed for him.

"All you want," he said again, "is to be able to say to somebody, *anybody* at the end of your life: '*This* is what I have done. *This* is what I have accomplished.'"

And that was when he really lost it. Crying, heaving, snot and everything. Mr. Westerburg dropped his forehead to the table, which was sticky, probably from him spilling drinks all over the place. He jerked his arm and his drink looked like it was gonna jump out of the glass and onto my shirt. I put my hand on his shoulder to stop it from happening … which must've made him feel better because, next thing I knew, my teacher passed out right there on the tabletop, with a drink in one hand and a cigarette in the other.

I put his cigarette out in the ashtray. I went around to his side of the booth. I dug his car keys out of the hip pocket of his jeans, pulled his wallet from the inside of his coat, found his driver's license, then put the wallet back.

The bartender came around with his refill, stopped, and put her free hand on her hip. I handed her Mr. Westerburg's keys and his driver's license, and then I gave her all the money I had, which was probably about twenty bucks. And I asked her to call him a taxi, to give the cabbie Mr. Westerburg's keys, to pay him with my money to go to the address on the license.

"Poor sap's been here all night," she said, nodding at the money. "'Least he cleared his tab 'fore he passed out."

"There's that," I said. "Happy Thanksgiving," and I got out of that place as fast as I could.

I went home and sat in front of the TV in the living room. That same movie from the pub was just ending: The guy from the bathroom came back from the dead and was eating the brains of the brother of the guy who had shot him: The End. Then the news, and then that ended. I hit the off button on the remote and sat there completely in the dark.

I remember thinking about what Mr. Westerburg had said, about knowing that I'd get into college and everything. For some reason, I was a lot more hopeful *before* he'd said it. I mean I'd already practiced how I would casually read the letter out loud late one night when Mom'd had a particularly bad time at work. I had no idea about the guy being a priest. Priests should never be alone on Thanksgiving, I don't care if they're still priests or not. Thanksgiving—what a joke. People should never have to drive their drunk mother home then carry her in, especially not on Thanksgiving. I wished I could've been as sure of myself as Mr. Westerburg had been, but the funny thing was, I *had* been. I *had* been, before I had to make sure he didn't try driving off somewhere and wrap his car around the trunk of a tree.

Jesus Christ. It wasn't midnight yet, but I needed to lie down, I was shaking. I mean, I was *shaking*, I couldn't help it. I kept thinking about school, how I'd have to go back there on Monday, how I couldn't face Mr. Westerburg, I couldn't face anybody, not like this. I thought about my mother tomorrow morning, and I wondered if she would be able to tell that somehow she had ended up completely disappointing me, that even if I did go to college and become a dentist, I couldn't help but eventually disappoint her.

Man, was I *depressed*. I went to bed, tossed and turned for a while before I fell asleep and had a dream—there was Mr. Westerburg, throwing up all over the table at that pub, talking about how one person cannot possibly something or the other. The zombie from that movie sitting in the booth behind him, spooning the brains out from a hole in the top of my father's skull. Bob Dylan in the corner singing a duet with Socrates about the trouble with syllogistic logic. The bartender licking her boyfriend's fingers over and over again, when I heard something that didn't exactly fit.

I need something that you got: That's what I heard. I heard it and I woke up just in time to hear it again. Must've been four in the morning, and it wasn't until it was too late that I realized she wasn't in her own bed. *I need something that you got*—I just lay there with my arms to my side like I was still asleep and I kept thinking about Hamlet and Mr. Westerburg and gym class, and Socrates, how maybe those young boys had had something that he'd needed too. Socrates, I kept on thinking, over and over again in the dark, my mind in a loop, maybe those young boys … when I heard my mother whisper: *I love you, Joe.*

Marvin's Dilemma

It took the wind, dancing about the cabin before snapping out of the open window of a speeding limousine. It floated, it fell like a star, it flapped to a stop on the broad, black face of a man returning to his apartment, after an evening spent busting into and tearing apart the city arboretum.

Marvin pinched the dollar bill off his face, held it up high. And he shouted, because the only limo like this that he'd ever seen belonged to Mr. Booth, the man who'd cared enough about Marvin to toss him into detox, and then turned around and hired him. He waved the bill again and again, booming out his boss's name automatically, unable to stop himself even though it was precisely the sort of thing that had driven Jerry away.

Deep down, it was nearly impossible for Marvin to see himself any differently from the way that most others saw him: black dumb muscle, with an accent that hung on him like some thick coat made from the shadows of Atlanta. But Jerry? Jerry was smart. Jerry was small. Jerry was chestnut brown, from some unpronounceable place in Connecticut, and Jerry *loved* him.

He had a G.E.D., but only because Jerry had demanded it. Jerry, who'd finished college and was returning to school to be an anesthesiologist … and he'd get in and finish up and be great at his job too, Marvin knew. He had to. Yet he'd never felt that this man was slumming by being with him, only that he *himself* had been slumming, with everything he had done in his life before Jerry had come along. But how Jerry had accomplished this sleight of mind remained the biggest of mysteries to Marvin.

The first time they'd met was two years ago, and he was so clumsy that morning, knocking on Jerry's door with one hand while fumbling at his steel knuckles with the other. He'd worn a big brown coat to look more menacing, but the goddamned thing just kept getting in the way. The note Mr. Booth left earlier in the day said: "J. Cullen, #401. White walkup on the corner of Boylan/Hillsborough. Three weeks late. Make an example."

Jerry opened his door and Marvin slipped the knuckles off and into his pocket without even realizing it, immediately turning both gentle and polite. He heard himself kindly explaining that he was there on behalf of the landlord, to give Jerry an in-person reminder that he was three weeks past due … when Jerry invited him in for a cup of coffee.

Coffee was the last thing on his mind. But he went in anyway, and Jerry immediately complimented his accent. Jerry who, as he learned later, studied linguistics in college … Marvin had checked that space even more thoroughly than usual, suspicious of this little man, almost certain he was pulling something, that the real Jerry would leap out of a corner at any time, another coward needing to catch the big man by surprise. But the apartment was a studio, the kitchenette was in plain sight. The bathroom door stood wide open: There was no one else around. He heard a quick clink, but it was nothing more than a metal spoon in a porcelain mug.

Facing the sink, his back to Marvin, in the soft light cast by the sun through the open window beyond him,

Jerry promised to mail the check in the morning, and then he invited Marvin to dinner the following night.

Marvin blew vapor. He stuffed the dollar into his pocket and then plodded on down Hillsborough, thinking about Tennessee and what he'd found in the university library these past two weeks since Jerry had split for Nashville. The medical schools; the hospitals. The Grand Ole goddamned Opry. What else was there, what else would there ever be, in a place like Tennessee? "It's up to you," Jerry had said before leaving. "This time there is no one else to blame. No one left to make your choices for you."

It hadn't taken Jerry long to suss out what Marvin did for a living. And Jerry had mostly been fine with it ... until one night a couple of months ago, when Marvin came home with a scraped-up face from some easy side work. Jerry saw the scrape (Marvin didn't mention the bullets that had caused it) and went livid over the spot of blood. A decade earlier, as a teen, Marvin had fought two grown men and took a buck-knife twice in the shoulder, and he had never really given it a second thought, until then.

He turned the corner of Hillsborough and West opposite his townhouse and found dozens of people blocking the intersection. They were all headed to watch the Acorn drop at Moore Square: these grandparents and yuppies and done-up women, and squealing kids and swaddled infants. Quick loud couples, posing for cameras hung on the necks of others. One little girl, a doll in her arm, wheeling an elderly man down the middle of the street. He put his arm over the iron in his coat to hide the shape, and with the heel of his other hand hit the first warm door that he found, and he ducked inside.

Christmas lights were still up. A jukebox finished "Blue Eyes Crying in the Rain," then spun up something else that was lowdown and depressing. Fake fire, creaking yellow lights in dusty plastic logs, lit the corner beneath a plaster chimney. The bartender, the only other body there, stood hunched in the back of the room, eyed Marvin up and down, and kept on sweeping. The walls were black, the floor an ashen tone that never cleans well, the counter up so high that when Marvin took a stool, he thought he'd fallen to the floor … and the whole place smelled of mice. The words on the mirror past the bottles of liquor read the name of this sad little place, and when it was established.

Marvin yanked all of the money out of his pockets and made a big show of splashing the change on the metal counter. The bartender took his time putting up the broom, yet Marvin didn't mind: he only sighed, looking at the money. Remembering how, at the beginning, he'd thought Jerry had the smell of the beach in his hair. But that scent had turned out to be everywhere, all over him. During sex Marvin could taste it, better than his previous boyfriend, who'd tasted only of scorched coffee.

Last year for Christmas, Jerry had given him a hardback dictionary and made him promise to read it cover to cover, and Marvin had opened the pages, and the words themselves had smelled like this. He remembered this summer solstice, he and Jerry and the endless final hour of the longest day of a beautiful year, which they'd spent in the arboretum that he, tonight, had savaged beyond repair. But the pastel light and flowers that day, he suddenly wondered: Had they also carried this scent? Had even that day when he first met him been soaked in the freshness of the sea, or was he now just confused and remembering things how he wanted, not as they had occurred?

From some distant land, the voice of every jackass bartender Marvin had ever met demanded what he wanted to drink. And Marvin closed his eyes, balled his fist, brought it down like a feather to the countertop, and whispered: "The ocean." He then raised the bill to his face and breathed in, imagining:

you knock on the door
he opens it
his eyes, your shield:
you have failed at being a shadow
the moment you cannot see past it
the things that you remember

(he had said this once, and it was only now that Marvin was figuring it out)

they are as permanent
and lasting
as the waves
of the ocean

"The ocean." Marvin says it again, pocketing the dollar. He kicks his chair over and leaves the coins on the counter.

His car is a couple minutes away if he runs and the crowd has thinned, which he does and it has. RDU is thirty minutes from here, but he will make it in fifteen tonight, since Moore Square is downtown and his way is opposite the flow of traffic.

On the way to the airport, speeding along the interstate, he reaches into his pocket for the iron, which clinks like a spoon in a coffee mug when it meets the pitch-dark highway. A few miles later, Marvin parks and checks his watch: Three hours to go, and this will happen. He will spend the last minute of 1987 in his lover's arms.

The terminal whirs, attendants and handlers. Glassy pilots and taciturn fliers. Indifferent security. He has this sudden urge to ask each one—to go back to the people from the streets today and ask them, too—if, when they shut their eyes at night, who they are and where they want to be comes at them like a beam of light in the dark. The ticket Marvin buys with a stolen card, the card he then tosses into a bathroom stall.

He walks past gate after gate, through the long hallways between them, along facades of roped-off shops and sealed-up restaurants. To A10, Delta to Atlanta then Nashville then God-knows-where. There is, behind the counter, an Asian woman with long gray hair and a puffed-out face. Beyond her is a blonde in a white Oxford and faded jeans, facing a large window and holding paper money loosely in her hand. One of maybe a thousand passengers Marvin has seen thus far.

He goes to the counter and gets a boarding pass from the Asian woman, who doesn't say anything. He walks over to the window, next to the blonde, realizing then that it's a boarding pass, not money, that she is holding. After a long while, they look at one another as if to say something, but are quickly interrupted by the sharp roar of turbine engines.

A pale blue 727 drifts toward the tarmac. Marvin and the girl, whose name is Carolyn, they quit breathing to keep from fogging the window. The aircraft holds steady above ground before swinging hard, around and back again, in a tight arc.

A man with cleaning fluid and a rag shoos the pair from the glass, cleans it, then disappears. At the entrance to the Jetway Marvin glances at his watch, and it is 10:01 p.m. ... but not in Nashville. He knows time now, better than he ever did before. He knows that it is an hour earlier there. On Jerry's time, he will meet the New Year in Tennessee.

Carolyn waits behind him. Somewhere inside of her real home, her recently widowed mother is sitting at a bay window with her eyes closed, her thoughts in the east even while facing the Pacific. In little more than five hours, she will answer the doorbell, and her hands will tremble at the sight of her daughter standing there.

Fifteen minutes pass, and a chime sounds. Carolyn and Marvin walk past the ticket taker, stepping quietly through the Jetway and into a cabin at two-thirds capacity. Carolyn's seat is next to his; she touches the Plexiglas window and looks outside. She is wondering if there will be food on this flight because that hot dog those hours ago won't last, as attendants mime procedure, and the reading lights begin to glow.

Urania's Mirror

When Urania's bell worked, when it came with a report, she wanted to hear it. She *loved* to hear it, this bell that was less tone than feeling, rippling along her spine like water trickling down the throat of a bone-dry riverbed. Each user's bell was unique so when things went right, when it came with a report, Urania's bell was, for her, bold bursts of color by a window into the unknown, with intimations of both terror and delight.

But that was when it worked. Because the thing had just gone off *again*, snapping the girl awake at 5:00 a.m. And now she was sitting up in bed, looking for a report that she knew would never come, bitter at the empty promise of a broken bell.

These rings without reports ... As a tap nurse, Urania knew all too well what kind of a problem this was. Alerts and reports together were what pushed connections through the general network, across space and time, each user being their own node. Yet on rare occasions, especially with cheaper taps, you'd get a user experiencing rings without reports. Changes, maybe ... but what was the point of it all if the user could not track or see the results?

This specific glitch had affected Urania's tap a lot lately, waking her three times last week and twice the previous night. So she squinted now and tried to ignore it. She slipped out of bed, naked. She ate her meal squares so fast she nearly choked, then let the WC scrub her weary body down for the double at the clinic. Somewhere in all of this, the song of her broken bell went away.

Whenever Urania felt stressed, she tapped. When she grew bored or anxious, she tapped and although the job at the clinic had come with training that made her better at tapping than most, this hadn't resulted in habits that were any different than anyone else's. She walked down to Dale's for the usual fat cup of coffee, tapping as she waited in a line that was shorter than usual. She then spent the pressurized and silent, eastbound shuttle hurtling through the heavy murk of the city limits to its even darker center, where her clinic was, lost in deep remembering ... though, through tapping, this was less reassembly and more revision. *Life*, but lived in four-dimensional space.

Hazy strings, these were, when unassisted: desiccated elements of a trip with her mother twelve years ago, when Urania was only seven, to the Goodlands on the northern California coast. Individual strands, faces and feelings and notions afloat like the loose ends they were, in a pulsating wind. Sometimes touching, yet never seeming to touch the same way twice. But when she centered herself within the tap, she was there again, reliving it. At the beginning of a unified thread of a day and at the end of it, one smooth and twisted loop of all at once.

And with her skill and talent and training, so was the rest, all of it in granular detail: Urania's mother Debbie, the soft and raw blonde who'd died while dreaming a few months later. Uncle Randy from southern Oregon, who'd raised his baby-sister's kid the best he could after Debbie passed in the night, and when Urania grew up and ran off to the city, he stayed behind in that ancient log cabin. His two buddies from college, too, were there that day on a beach that was hot and kinetic, the sea breeze soaked in silk and sweat; graying geneticists who'd adopted, late, two siblings from out past the catchment because they'd never been able to conceive on their own. Their boy Luis, who graduated as an orbital designer just twenty-four months before dying of stroke late last year, in the sleeping car of a moon-bound shuttle. And his little sister Maria, pretty and five ... that small, raised mole on her right wrist. The tap reminding Urania that this poor little girl had also died recently, in one of the seedier sections of the orbiting ring.

Everyone and everything, good or bad, happy and sad: All right there or more precisely, right *here*, tendrils of connection stretched before and after them. Even the rainbow-themed cars of the train that schussed high above the beach party, tracing out the border of an ochre cliff that went up and away so dramatically that it seemed to never stop. The brown wagon, a single silver scratch on its driver-side door; a mechanized squirrel, frisky and gray with a puffball tail, arcing its wet nose at the buzzing train from the thinning boughs of a western hemlock—

Urania tapped further back.

She dropped into the sunnier part, she sped forward once again to the moment when the sun sagged through clouds and fell like a hot stone into the ocean, pressing the Pacific and everything else through its billowing screen of orange and blue. Waves that were black and green went brown again, a bruise that turned over onto itself as if there were something out in those waves, tumbling ... and Urania's body, in real time, began to slow. The shuttle, sensing its station.

There it went again, that broken bell again, annoying Urania, peaking inside her ears. She had to listen, the pitch of the tune, she'd learned, "being deliberately set such that the user could not ignore the audition." She winced, wishing only that it would *mean* something again, this singing that didn't cease until the shuttle reached her stop, two blocks down from the clinic.

Tonight, she decided, slipping through the half-empty car. If this doesn't stop tonight, then it's an appointment for myself with Doc Fredrickson ... as she waved the door's vapor aside, alighting the shuttle.

*

From the shadowy safety of a corner-shop awning, a large young man in big black sweats scoped out his target: Tap nurse, tiny little thing, denim scrubs and a translucent mackintosh exiting the inbound lev. Long black curls and a rich complexion too, a bit rare these sunless days. Skin that looked warm in a way that he could almost smell, like beach sand in the early evening light. Emelie closed his eyes and whistled softly, *soto voce*, wishing he were close enough to scent her out. But when he looked again he edged back quickly, as his target turned and briefly trained her eyes upon him.

Emelie knew right off what she'd done, what *he'd* done. Her glance was incidental, something passengers naturally do after stepping through the vapor from the doors. And yet he'd reacted instinctively as if she had actually seen him, and now he felt the old, familiar shame. A girl this beautiful ... they never truly saw a heavy man, not these days, even if they happened to fall out of tap and look his way. He hated hearing this, but it was true what the handlers often told him, that a childhood spent as a fat kid, the root of his "talent" for invisibility, was precisely what made Emelie such a great field agent. He reached up distractedly; he ran the knuckle of his thumb around the circular scar at the base of his chin. A cigar burn, where the touch of someone who mattered had never been.

It continually shamed him that even the tiniest part of himself still held on to the way he'd once felt, the way that he used to be. Endlessly vulnerable, so beholden to the vision of the blind. He'd lost enough weight to be legal … and yet in his mind and soul, every phantom ounce remained, and this was something no tap could ever fix. Because they had never truly seen him, ever, and they never would. Even if he were tapped, even if he sent out a million contacts they still would not see him, these people who lived less in time than in dead and sunken memory. Even the cops, even the goddamned feds. Always glassy, always too glazed over to *see*.

He knew this all too well, and yet he still ducked whenever possible. Trailing this beautiful nurse who would find it impossible to see him even if she looked right at him, Emelie moved in the gray rain like a cloud unseen. He drifted in the nurse's wake, always no further than fifteen yards behind. She turned once to cross an intersection, which momentarily put them both out in the open … and Emelie's palms and pits began to sweat. In the middle of a busy street and he felt positively caged in, desperate for the comfort of corner, the safety of shadow.

He thought: Things are about to change.

*

He waited for her to walk into the clinic. He stood still as the gargoyle on the building opposite, in a drizzle that turned to rain that fell like iron filings on his face, and then he waited some more, until a minute past the appointment time and then another moment longer, to keep from standing out on the feeds. Inside, this clinic was the same as the other two he'd visited that day: lean and antiseptic open space, where everything that was white and clean nevertheless seemed smeared, as if all of these flat surfaces had been slathered in the thing a person loses the moment they die, or get tapped. Numerous stubby hallways, each leading to more of the same. Emelie shook his shaggy head without shaking it.

"Name?"

The receptionist, her voice acid on a copper plate. Glasses that were purely decorative, one lens so big she seemed miles ahead of it.

"Jeffers," he said, "Angus Jeffers."

"Jeffers, ten a.m. appointment." The old lady aimed an eyebrow at the clock floating between them and swabbed him for his payment and metrics. She then handed him over to somebody else, a thin girl with indigo hair and a voice like lukewarm water. Three stout hallways down to a small examination room, with soft swing music piping from the walls.

The girl with the hair introduced him to his nurse, the target he'd followed inside and at long last, for one far-too-brief moment, Emelie let his eyes run free, he let them have their way with her.

The communiqué had detailed OORT's surveillance and observation, months of it, mostly through hacked feeds, of this one and the other two from the earlier clinics. But the target was alone with him now, in person ... and she seemed so small, so defenseless in their private chamber, with a chair and a screen and a bed and a thin, Japanese divider. He breathed in and those other two, he suddenly realized: They'd smelled alike, yet so different from this one. Much less ... naïve.

"Angus?" Urania said, and he nodded, kept his big head down, took a small step back: this to draw her to him. There was still the other one, with the hair, he considered briefly. You could jog down the hall and finish this that way ... but the idea was gone almost as soon as it had arrived.

She waved off the music and came forward. She reached for his deliberately trembling hand, and Emelie thought: That's it. You can leave this fucking place now. Yet he didn't move.

"The procedure won't hurt," she said. "Well ... not much."

"Some kinda promise?" he asked, using the same nervous smile he'd used earlier that day, at the other clinics. "It's not a terribly good one."

She smiled back, though only halfway. Too young, he reckoned quickly, for repartee. "Don't you worry," she said. "Though with your size ... "

Emelie looked at his shoes again; Urania reached for his hand again, thereby infecting herself twice.

"You're fine," she promised. "It's close, I admit, but you're within BMI and I've done doubled taps before. All us nurses have."

You're a bastard, Emelie thought, trying and failing to look the girl in the eye.

"Now, when you're ready, take your shirt up and lie facedown here. Soon you'll just flick a switch inside, and it'll be like picking up a really good book, the best you ever read. All your memories, even the connections between them. And then there's how the whole world just ... opens up. Like a little flower does, when the people in your life start letting you in."

The people in my life ... Emelie reached again for that nervous smile. He knew the training these tap nurses received, he'd seen the scripts. Alone together and she still couldn't *see* him, and none of this was coming natural to her. But he was starting to see the truth of it, that the soul of this poor young girl, the spirit of the woman she might become, was immaterial to the very people that he busted his ass for, the ones that he was so busy risking his own life for. All to prove one point, *their* point: that tapping was tearing the world apart.

Those were the people in his life.

The whirring burr of a tap-setter, spinning down a rig customized to his metrics and price point. "Your back," she said finally. "You might be sore there when we finish, for like a week. But after that? Your brain'll be different, *better*." Urania rounded the shōji for her kit, pinching the button on her scrubs for the sanitizing gloves ... though by then, those gloves were useless.

When she stepped back around the shōji, gloves on and kit in hand, the girl met only cool air and empty space.

*

An hour later she was at her bathroom mirror, blowing her nose and daubing at her nostrils. As was the case with most residents of the city, it had been many years since Urania had had a cold. She swung the mirror open and held her arm out into the pharmacy's well.

A silver dial spun. The AI's voice directed her to try again in the morning: "an early-stage viral infection," it said, one so mild that there was no reason to rush. She cursed twice, blew her nose several times.

In her living room, Urania ordered the AI in the mirror there to re-run the diagnostic but got the same answer as before, and she breathed out heavily, grabbing the mirror's long curving frame to slam it shut … then stopped short. Thick green glass and a silver frame, the mirror had belonged to her mother Debbie, a long time ago. The one thing from Uncle Randy's that she'd kept after he died, but he was gone now and it was only making Urania feel worse to remember him.

She curled up on her couch and jumped into her tap, desperate for a distracting memory, anything bright enough to turn her away from how she was feeling. But her bell again. That song again … only this time, *with* a report.

She punched it up anxiously. Saw the little boy's face. "Jayson," said the name on the report. Riding shotgun in that same electric wagon from her childhood vacation in the Goodlands, the Subaru that was, for now, matching the lev train's speed and she could swear she knew the name, recognized its printed shape. But how had she never tapped this connection before?

She clicked again and saw the shifting image of a badge. She knew the name, those long white feathers on brown and stippled synthetic skin. "Dale's" in flashy cursive along the bottom, same kid. That scar on his chin, those nervous eyes. Urania could not believe that she had never *seen* from this place before.

So she squeezed herself thin, working the network for a span of time that she did not feel, right up to the eighteen-hour limit. Until she grayed out, until the night itself devoured her.

*

Morning came, rainier than ever. She ignored the pharmacy. She tapped in sick, waited for the storm to flag.

She swaddled herself in Angora; she slipped on an old-style Argos cap and told her tap to play the audio from the last time she'd listened to music in the sun: *In the Wee Small Hours*, a favorite of Uncle Randy's. Three months ago in Meadowland Park, the dying hours of a cool, muted summer, with some boy she no longer cared to remember. Urania heard the rain ease then labored three miserable blocks, down to the corner of Wiggins and Dale.

Dale's had been her favorite café since getting to the city. Fresh coffee wasn't cheap, but Dale's was reasonably priced and besides, this habit of her uncle's was Urania's now. She'd worked hard last night to realize that at the center of this new mystery was a boy who'd been a barista at Dale's almost as long as she'd been a customer there.

She liked the way he looked.

Big kid, blade of a smile, cutting the air the way moonlight does through a cornice of snow. Cheekbones like ridges in his hill of a face. Thin lips in that rosewood-colored rise, hard as marble, handsome … but how Jayson looked was not why she'd trudged down here, with a communicable infection and in the rain.

Because she'd seen the outlines of it: the sister, three years older, raped when she was seventeen. Numerous arrests for him afterward as a juvenile, for assault. The night he'd held up that corner store in Weed, the long hike north and east, to this city where he'd lived ever since. The last time his mother wrote, the letter telling how his dad had disappeared with a woman he'd met in the fields, and now she was alone and most nights, the sister was nowhere to be found.

Shapes were what she had seen. And it had shocked Urania last night to realize how much she wanted to see more, to *know* more of this stranger who'd smiled at her so many times, even if she'd only passively realized it and hence hardly returned it. So today she waited her turn, until he looked up again and smiled again. And she touched his hand quickly and for the very first time, without asking.

Late that night came her bell inside, thrilling her with its report: *Jayson.* She banged her elbow hard at the sound, against her nightstand ... but the pain eased when she saw the color code. Bright red, all lines pushed up-network. He was letting her *in.*

Urania clicked the report, brought it up. Saw each pore of every face that he'd bashed in, in those months after the rape. Beating each and every one into the rusty dirt of their shared mountain town, for the awful things they'd said about his sister, about what had happened. And Urania felt, with every blow, that burnt-sienna blend of rage and self-hatred that had overcome him; the stretches of time he'd spent locked up; those long hours and days alone, gray rooms and gray windows into skies that were themselves great spans of sheet metal.

She heard the other boys in the detention center, egging on the brown kid, the one who would end up dead from taking shots of the oral pain meds they'd stolen from the pharmacy and were daring him to take ... and Urania felt the guilt that Jayson still wrestled with for not stopping them. She felt a lot of guilt, the long dreadful reach of it, from Jayson. She saw the robbery, felt the plastic mask so hot and tight on his face, the fear and adrenaline and all that terrible, painful guilt rising like a lead bubble the morning after ... and suddenly knew why he'd boxed up the money and the gun and the mask and mailed it all back to the store—

She wanted *more*.

*

Some dreams, they never end.

They last four long years or two short hours or ten brief minutes, during which two young people manage to spend their entire lives together. Coupled in quantum entanglement, they are unified strings before they meet.

Coincident since both were children. Two lightly polished marbles, momentarily touching as they swing through space and time. Fruits of the same ground, opposing sides of the same green road that still zippers the same old valley, in the same square block of one melancholy mountain town. Jupiter and Mars, a giant and a stony place: They were in alignment that day, on a beach where a girl turns her gaze inland just as a little boy and his migrant-farmer parents happen to be racing by.

Urania returned to Dale's the next day feeling much improved, without the help of her pharmacy. And he was there, just another kid who'd run away from their hometown for the city, when he was seventeen. Not working, just ... sitting there, on a stool at a table as if he were a customer. As if waiting for her, as if after last night she'd become the most basic of eventualities. No uniform, no badge. She walked a straight line toward him.

And he smiled. Before either had said a word, he handed her a plastic sleeve. Inside was an eight-by-eleven sheet of parchment, thick and torn at the edges. Virgo, wings and sandals and a striped, flowing dress. Her sign, from the ancient star chart that had given Urania her name. She eased the plate back into the envelope and sat down, pressing it flat to the table.

"Stop grinning," she said softly. "Unless you want me to hate you."

*

Four years. Four incredibly happy years.

Four years and two children, a boy and a girl, both born after the big escape from that miserable city. She and Jayson met six months before packing up and moving back to the little town in southern Oregon where they'd grown up, into the old log cabin Uncle Randy had left her, in the holographic will he'd penned shortly before jogging off into the woods, stopping at a clearing near the California border, and setting himself on fire. Their kids were born at home, in that cabin ... and the minutes and hours, days and years, lurch forward.

Luis and Maria ... but who were these kids that she loved so much? Luis, who would become an orbital designer just two years before breaking Urania and Jayson in two by dying of stroke, on a moon-bound shuttle: their mother's tap showing her this boy, *her* baby boy, the way the crew had found him, frozen from a spasm that left him shaped like a question mark. And little Maria! Her sweet baby! That small mole on her right wrist! Tapping showed the daughter too, but at the very end. Only that fat, hooded figure emptying her pockets, taking the drugs and tickets and money, fading into black and leaving Maria for dead out there, in the seediest reaches of the orbiting ring—

A shaking spread. The vanishing years, those long and lost hours, seeking themselves minute by minute, folding into one another until Urania's tap slipped quickly into nothing at all.

*

Awake again, this time to the pricked, stretched feeling of needles and tubes in her arms. Light chatter in the air and a white, flat light making a grounded emptiness of wherever she was. She breathed in, sussing out the scent of the cabin that it often seemed she'd always called home. She wanted Jayson … but this thing in her throat. Someone, a bright-white bulb, leaned over and began easing it out.

"Stay still," a voice ordered. Even breathing hurt. She tried, failed, to tap.

Another voice said, "Don't. You'll rip out your cords if you try." Then, "You got them levels?"

"Yup. Coming down, fast. She's with it."

"Two weeks," muttered another, with spit and pity in her voice. "Good grief."

"Don't know about 'good,'" the first one said. "It's sure powerful, though. This one, she had to yank her own governor to tap this long. Pulled it clean out of her spine, with just a razor and a pair of needle-nose—"

"*Jesus*. So she's on an ungoverned tap, with signal branched out well beyond the occipital lobe."

"Levels are officially down," the third one said. "I better run and find the guy paying us to bring her back."

She whispered the names of her kids and husband and no one heard, no one said anything in return. She tried tapping again but felt like a drowning swimmer, reaching for a hand that kept pulling out of reach. What *was* this? "Who are you?" one asked slowly, his voice muted as if speaking through plastic. "What's your name?" "Where are you?" questions that grew slower and closer, all muted. More and more of it, until one voice quieted the rest.

"Tell me," he said, "about your baby girl."

Warm calloused hands, taking one of hers. "The beach," he said, and he sounded like somebody that she used to know. "Three weeks ago, we lost her there. Your little girl went out for a swim and never came back in. But you don't remember ... or you won't remember. Dear God, why would a mother *want* to?"

He had taken her by the shoulders and was now raising her to a seated position. He touched his sister's chin, turning her face toward the mirror, the large one in a chrome frame on the wall beside her. A bell, the cabin's old-fashioned landline, began to ring and Randy and the doctor and all those tap nurses stood there ignoring it, saying nothing. Waiting for Debbie's vision to clear, for her to *see*.

About the Author

A published scholar and fiction writer, Ulrick Casimir lives, writes, and teaches on the college/university level in the Pacific Northwest. Ulrick earned his BA from North Carolina State University and an MFA in Creative Writing from the University of North Carolina at Greensboro; he also holds an MA and a PhD, both in English, from the University of Oregon, where for the past several years he has taught writing and film for the English department and for Clark Honors College. Ulrick's scholarly work has appeared in the film journal *Jump Cut*, and his short fiction has most recently appeared in *Plainsongs*. *Children of the Night* is his debut story collection.

Connect with Ulrick on social media:
    Facebook: @UCasimir
    Twitter: ulrickcasimir
    Instagram: MyBlackNoir
    Web: ulrickcasimir.com

CPSIA information can be obtained
at www.ICGtesting.com
Printed in the USA
FFHW021717050319
50884570-56286FF

9 780999 686928